LOVE AND MAGIC

LOVE AND MAGIC

FOUR DELIGHTFULLY SPUN YARNS

JOHN HANLON

WOVEN WORDS
Auckland, New Zealand

Publisher: Woven Words

Author website: www.johnhanlon.co.nz

A catalogue record for this book is available from the National Library of New Zealand.

Contents

LOVE AND MAGIC

———

Kate watched Brad swaggering towards her and was seized by an all too familiar sense of panic. Mercifully, she was granted a few moments' reprieve when he stopped to talk to a small group of their guests. She was standing next to the musicians — two old men attacking violin and accordion with gusto — so she couldn't hear what he was saying, but she didn't need to; she knew it would be tactless, peppered with sexual innuendo and more than likely embarrassing for those forced to listen. A few watery smiles rippled around the group as if to confirm this.

She sighed and let her gaze wander outside to where a soft drizzle was catching the fire of the setting sun. The beauty of it brought her no comfort.

'Outside! You must be mad. It'll rain for sure,' Brad ranted

when she told him she planned to hold his birthday party in the garden.

Far from being disappointed that the rain had arrived, he'd be delighted to be proven right. She dreaded the thought of his gloating.

Her gloomy thoughts were interrupted by a sudden hush in the conversation. She looked up to see a strange bat-like silhouette standing in the main entrance to the marquee. It appeared to flare its wings to shake off a fine spray of raindrops before entering in a swirl of black.

Under lights the new arrival was revealed to be a hunchbacked man dressed in a dinner jacket, bow tie and black cape. And despite the initial pity one might feel at the sight of a body so twisted and bowed, it was plain to see this man wasn't bowed in spirit. Pride and intelligence emanated from his keen green eyes as he scanned their faces.

When he saw Kate, he smiled, and moved towards her.

The others fell into curious silence. Even the musicians stopped playing and watched in fascination as this odd character shuffled across the marquee like a hermit crab.

When he was a few feet from her, he slowly stretched out an arm and, with a snap of his fingers, produced a beautiful bunch of white carnations.

He offered them to her.

Everyone gasped and smiled in the way they do when magic is performed before their very eyes. They gathered closer.

The man's skin was olive and impossibly smooth, giving him an almost polished look. His black eyebrows, which swept back precisely at the base of his high forehead, looked so symmetrical Kate thought for an instant they might be painted on — then she noticed a small scar in the right one and was almost relieved to find it there. His nose, too, was imperfect, bending off to one side above a decidedly sensuous mouth.

She brought her gaze back to his steady green eyes and saw that they now held a look of warmth and amusement. And there was something else ... something familiar. A shadow stirred, briefly, in a rarely visited part of her memory — then it was gone.

Ignoring the curious onlookers and Kate's unblinking scrutiny, the man in black continued to hold the flowers out to her. He encouraged her to accept them with a slight raising of his eyebrows and a mischievous smile.

Kate was convinced that the moment she reached for them, the carnations would be transformed into a rubber snake or something equally horrific. She thought this because she knew he had to be 'Mahmoud the Magnificent', the magician she'd booked after finding his leaflet in the letter box on the very day she decided she'd have live entertainment at Brad's birthday party.

'Please, Mrs Warren, the flowers are for you,' he said.

His voice was warm and slightly accented and she knew she'd never heard it before, yet the feeling that she knew him persisted. However, this was no time to go in pursuit of an elusive memory; everyone was willing her to accept the flowers. Not wishing to spoil their fun (after all, she had hired the fellow to entertain), she reached out fearing the worst.

Nothing happened. No trick, no rubber snake. Much to her surprise and delight the flowers proved to be real. 'Thank you,' she said with obvious relief. 'I love carnations.'

'I know,' he said. 'They're your favourite flowers.'

'How could you possibly know that? And how on earth did you know I was Mrs Warren?'

'Mahmoud knows.'

'Yeah, well, I'd like to know who the hell Mahmoud the chocolate Quasimodo is!' Brad said as he shoved forward to stand possessively by her side.

Their guests fell into an embarrassed silence.

If the magician was insulted, he didn't show it. 'Please allow me to introduce myself. I am Mahmoud the Magnificent, here at the request of your charming wife to entertain you on the occasion of your thirty-seventh birthday.'

He held out his hand.

Brad ignored it.

Kate saw that the hand was horribly scarred; two of the fingers appeared to be webbed together. She found herself imagining that hand sliding across her breast and shuddered unwittingly.

Mahmoud quickly withdrew the hand from her sight.

She blushed. Surely he couldn't have known?

Brad noticed none of this. 'Mahmoud the Magnificent, my arse. More like Willie the Wanker if you ask me,' he said and laughed.

Nobody else seemed amused.

Mahmoud smiled whimsically. 'Ahhh yes, the clothes … I am a bit overdressed, I admit. It is a necessary part of the act, I'm afraid.'

'Need plenty of pockets to hide things in, eh?' Brad sneered. He addressed this last remark to the others, not the crippled magician.

They smiled helplessly.

Kate was puzzled: how had Mahmoud known it was Brad's thirty-seventh birthday? She'd only told his agent it was a birthday party; she hadn't said *whose* birthday it was, and no age had been mentioned. He must have asked someone outside before he made his grand entrance.

Brad was talking at her. 'You never said anything about a magician. Tents, magicians, what next — the whole bloody circus?'

The others began to shuffle about uncomfortably. There was a time when Brad's jibes had been amusing, but nowadays they were just bitter and belligerent. His public bullying of Kate was something even his oldest friends were finding impossible to cope with. Kate implored them to ignore it — assuring them it was only the alcohol talking, that she didn't take it to heart and neither should they. But such behaviour is hard to ignore or forgive.

And tonight, despite the occasion, Brad was at his worst: 'Speaking of tents and circuses,' he persisted, 'I told you having the party outside was a shit-house idea. I knew it'd rain.'

Although she'd been prepared for this, Kate hadn't been able to think of a suitable reply.

Mahmoud came to her rescue. 'There is no rain,' he said.

Everyone turned to look outside to what was now a perfect afternoon. Magically, the drizzle and clouds had disappeared.

They looked back at Brad.

'Yeah, well ... lucky for you,' Brad grunted at Kate as he jostled his way outside to assure himself that the rain had really gone.

'Lucky for all of us, I think,' Mahmoud smiled at Kate. 'Now perhaps I can perform my show outside in your lovely garden.'

So saying he scuttled past Brad out into the sunlight.

Kate followed slowly, still puzzled by the certainty that she'd met this fascinating fellow somewhere before.

The others drifted out after her, buzzing excitedly.

Brad was less than enthusiastic. 'I bet this is costing me a fortune.'

'I'm paying,' Kate assured him, expecting no thanks.

Brad ignored her and went to join the others. As he reached the edge of the small crowd that had gathered around the magician, he threw his arm around their neighbour, Tammy Anderson, and drew her roughly into his side. As subtly as she could, Tammy tried to break away, but Brad held her firmly. She looked back helplessly at Kate, who smiled and shrugged. There was nothing she could do. They were both trapped. For Tammy it would only be for a few uncomfortable minutes; for Kate it had been years.

Although most soon realise the folly in it, few women could honestly say they survived their younger years without experiencing at least a quickening of the heart in the presence of that confident and often envied male creature who, by virtue of looks, personality, strength or athletic ability, is acknowledged by all others to be 'the leader of the pack'.

In Kate's case, this affliction had been rather more permanent.

It began one summer in a sunburned beach resort where a high school dropout by the name of Brad Warren had been the undisputed king of the beach. Bronzed, blond, muscular and relaxed, his roguish blue eyes and disarming smile were irresistible to any girl in search of summer romance.

Kate had never seen eyes so blue, or eyes that could promise so much in a single glance.

And as if looks, wit and charm weren't enough, he also played lead guitar with a popular band and sang with a hard-edged voice that stirred her very soul.

From the very first time she saw him, Kate was smitten.

And she wasn't alone in her infatuation; the competition for Brad's attentions that summer was fierce. Scores of intelligent, free-spirited girls were reduced to little more than fawning groupies at the mere mention of his name. The lengths they went to to attract his attention bordered on the ridiculous. Kate, herself, was one of the worst.

It was all to no avail, because for most of that summer he ignored her and chose instead the abundant curves and accommodating disposition of a peroxided blonde by the name of Pauline Luke (or 'Puke', as she was unkindly referred to by those who envied her, which included virtually every female for twenty miles in any direction).

Then, one fateful night late in January, Brad abandoned Pauline and claimed Kate. There is no other way to describe what happened.

The last dance for the holiday break had ended. The band was packing up and everyone who mattered was heading for a bonfire party on a small beach a few miles up the coast. There was a touch of sadness about the night — by noon the next day, the Romeos and Juliets of the tented villages and caravan parks would be torn apart as fate and family returned them to homes and lives far from each other. For friends and lovers alike, it was a time for tearful goodbyes and heartfelt promises that could never be kept.

Kate and her friends — many of whom had remained depressingly unattached for the entire holiday break — were standing in front of the local hall hoping to hitch a ride to the beach party. Cars cruised by like chrome-toothed sharks, and hanging from their windows were all the young men who would never be Brad Warren. Accepting a ride with any of these hormone-crazed youths was sure to involve at least a minor tussle with a nervous hand in search of a willing breast. For this reason, among others, the girls had wisely agreed to stick together. They were dallying with an overly zealous red-haired boy called Ralph — who had the use of the family station wagon for the night — when the door to the hall opened and Brad emerged with guitar case in hand and Pauline Puke following a few steps behind. Pauline was crying: 'I'm sorry, Brad. I don't know why I said that. It must have been the wine ... I didn't ... please ...'

One look at Brad's face told you Pauline's pleading was wasted. None of them knew what she had done and none of them cared. Without a second thought for the poor girl's shattered heart, every young woman there realised with predatory glee that Pauline was past tense and the road to dreamland was open.

The night held its breath.

Brad surveyed the weak-kneed feminine huddle before him. Their eagerness was transparent.

After the longest minute, he stepped forward, looked directly at Kate and held out his hand. As if hypnotised, she went to him and fell naturally in by his side. No words were exchanged, none was needed; so complete was her infatuation that a look, a smile and an extended hand were all that she asked for and more than she'd dreamed of. He claimed her and she acquiesced almost gratefully. Such was the seduction of Kate Hamilton.

Theirs was no ordinary short-term summer romance. It proved deep, lasting and wonderful. Kate couldn't believe she could be so happy for so long. He was the hero and she was his lady. They were the perfect couple. Everyone agreed.

Two years later, when he asked her to marry him, her heart sang.

She was only nineteen and he barely twenty-three.

Her mother cried and her father tried not to get angry. 'The boy's a bloody pop singer, for Chrissake! How's he going to support you? Who does he think he is, Paul Lennon?'

'That's John Lennon, Dad.'

'I don't care if it's Rumplebloodystiltskin Lennon, at least he's making millions, which is more than can be said for this Brad whatshisname.'

In the end, however, her father relented and gave them his blessing along with a cheque for $5000, which was his last, if not most subtle, word on the subject.

A little over five years later, things began to fall apart.

It began when Brad came to understand, as many of us do, that time can be cruel to high school heroes.

For most of his early life he'd been the one others looked up to, the one they envied. He was the 'natural', the leader, the hero. Perhaps it was understandable, therefore, that he tended to dedicate himself to pursuits that came easily to him — sport and music — rather than academic subjects, which took time and hard work, and inspired little admiration from his peers. Besides which, he just couldn't see the point of burying himself in languages and logarithms, or the trials and tribulations of the British monarchy, when such things seemed so irrelevant in his view of the everyday world. So the day he turned sixteen he dropped out of school, leaving his friends to struggle on towards university while he enjoyed the fruits of a musician's life on the road.

For a few years, his lack of education hadn't mattered; he earned good money and had an enormous amount of fun doing it. Moreover, while the band enjoyed a heady time of popularity — aided immeasurably by his cavalier looks and riveting vocals — he was able to maintain his high profile and further cultivate the legend.

He was the one everyone wanted to be, or be with.

This is how it was the summer he met Kate.

In time, though, things began to change. His friends rarely came to the dances and clubs to cheer and envy him any more. They were moving on to new jobs, new interests and new friends. And on the odd occasions their paths did cross, while they always seemed genuinely pleased to see him, after a few minutes' reminiscing their eyes would begin to glaze over. Brad offered them little more than memories of another time — a happier, more carefree time, perhaps, but a time that was past, nonetheless. He had nothing to do with their present or their future.

On the other hand, he himself had no clear plans for the future. He knew by now it wasn't in the music business — he was good, but not *that* good. He needed something more substantial, something with long-term prospects; something he could rely upon and enjoy. Each day he scanned the newspapers for suitable opportunities; casually, though, as if checking his options rather than desperately searching for a future. He applied for a number of jobs, but could never get the ones he really liked.

Invariably, they were looking for people with higher qualifications than someone who'd left school at sixteen to sing in a rock band.

What made things worse was that he often found himself being interviewed by anal-retentive types he had always considered 'nerds' at school. Only now these same nerds held his future in their hands and it seemed to him that they used their power like a form of revenge. Each time he had to suffer their patronising rejections, he was seized by an overpowering desire to punch them. Unfortunately, these dark thoughts tended to show and, as the chip on his shoulder grew, his chances of being hired reduced.

The best he could manage were a few casual labouring jobs and a brief flirtation with a commission-only encyclopaedia-selling job that savaged his pride and earned him barely enough to pay the rent.

Then, inevitably, the band began to fall out of fashion. Bookings dropped off at a worrying rate.

In the end there were weeks when Kate's earnings as a receptionist in a real estate office were well in excess of his own.

Perhaps if he'd set his mind on some vocation, got in on the ground floor and worked his way up, things might have been different, but he found this impossible. To start at the bottom would mean ingratiating himself to lesser mortals in order to get ahead and he just couldn't do that.

Consequently, he was condemned by pride to remain on the outside looking in — with anger.

He was no longer the hero, no longer the one people envied. His glory belonged to another time — like a sports trophy that sits forgotten on the shelf except for those rare occasions when you take it down to remind yourself of a brief, shining moment that has gone for ever.

And the occasions when the old gang would get together to reminisce about Brad's glory days were becoming all too rare.

His legend was losing its shine.

While Brad may have mourned the passing of his prime, Kate did not. She loved the man, not the image. She was more than happy for him to remain a musician all his life, even a poor one, so long as it made him happy. She did, however, understand his torment. She knew how he hated to be beaten by anything or anyone. And — although he never discussed it — she knew that his sense of failure was beating him to death.

She tried to tell him it didn't matter — let the others have their heavily mortgaged homes, foreign cars and gold credit cards, she didn't need them. They had each other, they were happy, and that was all that mattered to her.

Brad didn't believe her. He was convinced she only said these things to make him feel better. He was certain that, like everyone else, she was merely patronising him.

This feeling only intensified when the real estate company promoted her to sales and she began to earn sizeable commissions. In one month she earned nearly double what he'd earned the whole of the previous year. Within two years she'd earned enough to put a deposit down on their house. Now she took care of the mortgage.

She wanted him to enjoy her success, to accept that her income enabled him to concentrate on his music; but all it did was increase his sense of failure.

Eventually, perhaps inevitably, the alcohol that had for so long fuelled his popular personality began to awaken a darker side to him.

Despite this, Kate tried to help — comforting him through bouts of paranoia and self-doubt, mopping up his vomit and enduring his depression.

But when the months turned into years, with each day bringing a new bout of drunken abuse, when she began to dread his foul-breathed, clammy-handed attempts at lovemaking, when her every gesture of love and support was hurled back at her in a self-pitying fury, she had to face the reality that there was nothing left worth saving.

Now, after two years of unremitting misery, she knew she had no choice but to leave him, and it was tearing her apart.

True to his stage name, Mahmoud was magnificent.

He began by moving among the guests performing a few simple sleight-of-hand tricks and some incredible feats of pickpocketing.

The late afternoon was filled with cries of amusement and delight as people discovered he had relieved them of their watch, or wallet, or belt, or — in one case — a bra.

At one point he stole Sally Baldwin's engagement ring and caused it to vanish before her eyes. He then produced an egg and assured her that the ring was inside it. But when he broke the egg into a glass bowl there was no sign of the ring. He seemed genuinely dismayed — the trick had always worked before. Sally looked worried. Her husband, Grant, was furious — the ring was worth a fortune. Things became decidedly tense until Mahmoud asked Grant to look in the pocket of his own jacket and, sure enough, there was the ring.

'Fuck me!' said Grant.

'No, thanks,' chorused the others, and hilarity reigned.

The only one not enjoying the show was Brad. During the search for the ring he had been shouting things like

'Look up his bum — I bet the poofter's hidden it up his ring-piece!' and other choice remarks along similar lines.

These witticisms were intended to unsettle the magician and amuse the others, but they failed in every respect.

Mahmoud alone appeared to accept it in good humour. 'So you think I'm a fake, Mr Warren?'

'I don't think so, mate, I know. This is no kiddies' party, you're out with grown-ups tonight.'

'Aaah ... yes. Children believe in magic, adults do not. That is a shame, don't you think?'

'Why? It's bloody reality, isn't it?'

'What is reality?'

'Wires, hidden trapdoors, mirrors. Trickery, mate — that's the reality.'

'Brad, please—' Kate tried to pull him away.

'It's quite all right, Mrs Warren,' Mahmoud assured her. 'Your husband doesn't believe in magic; this is cause for sadness, not anger.'

'You must be bloody joking!' Brad's blue eyes blazed indignantly. 'You feel sorry for me? Christ, mate, I should feel sorry for you — you pathetic hunchbacked coon!'

The bitterness of his insult stunned them all.

Only Mahmoud seemed unmoved. He looked thoughtfully at Brad as if reaching a decision of some kind.

The sun had dropped below the horizon and the crickets were beginning to serenade the twilight. One of the musicians, bothered by the strained silence, ventured a few nervous notes on his accordion, but a harsh glance from his violin-wielding partner silenced him.

No one spoke.

Mahmoud looked at Kate, sympathy filling his warm green eyes. 'It must be difficult to love a man who does not believe in magic.'

Brad took a threatening step forward. 'What kind of a—'

There was a blinding flash.

Brad leapt back in fright.

When the smoke cleared the magician had disappeared.

Some laughed. Some clapped. Brad looked bewildered.

'Looking for me, Mr Warren?' Mahmoud's voice came from within the marquee. As everyone looked in that direction he emerged, holding before him a large luminous orb — about the size of a basketball — which gave off a soft blue light.

'Nice trick, mate,' Brad said, having recovered his caustic composure. 'A bit of flash powder to divert our attention and you exit stage left. Clever, but not magic.'

Although they thought it unnecessary to say so, few would have argued with Brad's assessment.

Mahmoud seemed to sense what they were thinking and smiled. 'I see I have more than one sceptic in the audience tonight.'

They tried not to look guilty; they had no desire to insult the man, especially since he had developed his skills to such a degree despite his obvious handicaps. Then again, neither should he insult them by expecting them to believe what he did was really magic. It was illusion, nothing more.

'Well, then,' the magician grinned. 'I see I'm just going to have to convince you all.'

He had arrived at the party in a small truck painted midnight blue and covered in white and yellow stars of various sizes. 'Mahmoud the Magnificent' was painted boldly on each side panel in Superman-style lettering and there was a mobile phone number on the doors.

Surprisingly, for one so physically limited, he hadn't brought an assistant to help him. So he'd had to ask some of the guests to help him unload the truck and erect a small low stage in the garden.

Now that the day had settled into lingering twilight, the stage was largely in darkness and you could just make out the silhouette of a large trunk in centre stage, the folds of the gaudily painted canvas backdrop, and the shapes of a few props off to either side.

Holding the glowing orb in front of him, Mahmoud climbed awkwardly up onto the stage, hobbled to the centre of it and stood with his back to them. Then, balancing the orb on the fingertips of one hand, he slowly reached up until his arm was fully extended. Magically, the orb continued to rise, away from his outstretched fingers until it reached a point about eight feet above him. Here it stopped and hovered, its glow gradually intensifying until the entire stage was bathed in an eerie blue light.

He turned slowly and looked directly at Kate. 'I wonder what they'll make of that.'

Kate looked to see how her friends were reacting. They weren't. There was not a sound — not from them, nor the crickets, nor the birds, nor the neighbours. No children shrieking. No dogs barking. No traffic. It was as if the whole world was in suspended animation.

Except for her and Mahmoud.

'A cheap trick, I'm afraid,' the magician said as he hopped down off the stage, 'but I wanted to talk to you alone.'

Kate stared in horror at her motionless friends. 'What have you done to them? You've hypnotised me, haven't you? This is not happening. It's all in my imagination, isn't it?'

He was now standing close to her. 'Please don't worry, your friends are quite safe,' he assured her. 'They're lovely people, but I'm afraid, thanks to your husband, they're turning out to be quite a difficult audience.'

With an effort she dragged her eyes back to him. 'You did this because of Brad?'

'Well, he does seem determined to spoil his own party.'

'Yes, I'm sorry about that,' she said. 'Sometimes he gets a bit ... when he's had too much to drink, you know.'

'You love him very much, don't you?'

'I really don't think that's any of your business.'

'Perhaps not. However, if you're planning to leave

someone you love, I think somebody should make it their business.'

Leave someone you love — she felt her heart leap; how could he have possibly known that?

'Let's just say it's magic,' he said, reading her mind.

She found it hard to breathe, as if the air had turned to liquid. The man continued to invade her private thoughts in a way he had no right to.

'Look, Mahmoud, or whatever your real name is, you're a terrific magician. I respect that and I'm sure they do, too,' she said glancing around uncertainly at her inanimate friends. 'Why can't you leave it at that? Why is it so important that we believe what you do is *really* magic?'

'People who don't believe in magic cannot believe in love.'

'And *you'd* know, of course,' she said sharply — and immediately regretted her tone. It was too late. She saw that she'd hurt him in a way Brad had failed to. She began to apologise. 'Look, I'm sorry, I ...'

He was quick to recover. 'It's all right. It's my fault — I've been presumptuous.'

'Yes, you have. But ...' There was no way to undo what she'd said, no words to excuse it. She let it go.

Mahmoud gazed down at his scarred hand, turning it over slowly as if seeing it for the first time.

She noticed that he appeared weary, as if he were hunched by a huge weight on his shoulders rather than a cruel twist of nature.

When he spoke, his voice was quieter, less confident. 'I was in love, once. Platonically, of course, it has to be that way for me ...'

Kate softened. 'Did the girl know?'

'No.'

'Why didn't you tell her?'

'Would you, if you were me?'

She didn't answer.

He shrugged. 'The truth is, I never even spoke to her. I worshipped her from afar, as they say,' he paused, remembering. 'It was many years ago and in those days I was confined to a wheelchair.'

The familiar feeling returned to her again — a blurred image just out of reach. 'Were you afraid she'd be unkind?' she asked.

'No, she could never be unkind, it was not in her nature,' he said. 'She was a popular girl, a happy girl, I'd say, but her eyes were for the handsome boys, not for cripples.'

He said this without a trace of self-pity; it was simply an observation, a fact of life.

Kate could think of nothing appropriate to say.

'That's the reason I became interested in magic,' he said brightly.

She looked suitably mystified.

'I wanted to get attention, to become popular,' he explained. 'A fairly typical wish for a teenage boy, I think. And despite my handicaps, I was typical in most other respects. My first thought was to learn an instrument, but my hand made this impossible. So I chose magic instead.'

'But surely you need to be good with your hands to perform magic?'

'Yes, that's true. It was difficult for me, but I persisted. I found I had a gift for it. Besides, it's only sleight of hand that requires dexterity, not the kind of magic I perform.'

'Real magic, you mean.'

He smiled at the cynicism in her voice, but said nothing.

His calmness only served to further exasperate her. 'You're not going to start all that love and voodoo nonsense again?' she said.

'It's not nonsense — where there is love, there is magic; there can be no love without magic, and without love there is nothing.'

He was beginning to sound like a third-rate philosopher. 'Listen, the last thing I need right now is a guru. If you can read my mind — and you certainly appear to be able to — you'll know that love isn't exactly my favourite subject at the moment. Can't we just leave it alone?'

A look of rejection shadowed his deep-green eyes and for an instant he seemed quite helpless. She recognised that look — she had seen it before. But where? Something stirred and her resolve weakened. For some inexplicable reason, she felt the need to believe him — for his sake and her own. She reached out and took his deformed hand between both of hers.

'All right, if I say I *do* believe in magic, would it make any difference?'

'Only if you mean it.'

She sighed. 'I'd like to believe it, just like I'd like to believe in Santa Claus, UFOs and fairy godmothers — but how can I? I didn't stop believing in those things by choice, you know, I learned to. Life's like that. You find out the truth and you learn to live with the realities. There's no point wasting your life away waiting for miracles.'

'So you have no time for impossible dreams?' he said.

'No. Do you?'

He was looking down at her hands holding his. After a moment he looked up and she was struck, once again, by the cruel contrast between his handsome features and his distorted frame. 'Oh yes,' he said, almost in a whisper, 'I still have my dreams.'

'Well, it's time you learned that they're just that,' she said, 'just dreams. Sooner or later you have to grow up, face reality and get on with it, otherwise you'll just get left behind.'

'Like Brad?'

She let go of his hand and stepped back a pace in awe. 'You really are incredible, aren't you? The things you know ...'

He didn't say anything, but a feeling of deep compassion seemed to flow out of him and she was drawn to his warmth. He waited.

'I'm leaving him tomorrow,' she confessed.

'But you don't want to.'

'I can't stay. I'll only end up hating him.'

'He loves you, Kate.'

'He might have once,' she said. 'Now ...'

She looked across at Brad, the silence and stillness had taken the anger from him. There was a look of boyish wonder on his face. His blue eyes, so often narrowed in rage and despair, were wide, helpless and innocent. Her heart ached. 'You've seen what he's like. No one could put up with that.'

'I see only a man who has ceased to believe in his own magic.'

'Boy, you don't give up, do you?' she sighed.

'I only state what is true.'

'What if it is true? What can anyone do about it?'

'You must put the magic back into his life. And your own.'

'And you just happen to be giving away free samples tonight, right?'

'You might say that, yes.'

'You'll forgive me if I'm not convinced.'

'If I were to put the magic back into your marriage, would that convince you?'

She said nothing. She didn't need to.

'Then that is what I shall do,' he said.

Within seconds he was back on stage standing with his back to her staring up at the glowing orb. Slowly, he turned with his arms outspread and with a snap of his fingers brought the others back to life.

Completely unharmed, and oblivious to what had happened, they returned to oohing and aaahing and pointing at the floating orb.

Brad pushed his way right to the very front to make sure he got the best view.

'Aaah, Mr Warren,' Mahmoud said spying him. 'Perhaps you'd like to assist me with my next trick.'

'Want to stick a few swords through my head, eh?' Brad joked as he leapt onto the stage.

'No, but I would like to make you disappear,' Mahmoud smiled.

'Wouldn't we all,' someone yelled.

'Get stuffed!' Brad laughed, inverting a finger in the direction of the heckler.

Mahmoud walked over to a brightly painted box that stood on the left of the stage. It was about the size and shape of Dr. Who's telephone booth, which seemed appropriate when he explained what he intended doing.

'I will lock Mr Warren in here,' he said and, as quickly as his curious gait would allow, made his way across the stage and thumped on the lid of a large wooden trunk. 'And I will transport him through space to re-emerge in here.'

'That's what you think,' Brad grinned, his dazzling blue eyes more roguish than ever. He had no intention of co-operating in any way.

The crowd bubbled.

Mahmoud went back to the first box and held the door open.

Brad entered, sceptically. 'Prepare to make a dick of yourself, Mohammed,' he grinned. 'You can abracadabra till the cows come home, I'm not leaving this box.'

Mahmoud was undeterred. He closed the door on Brad's muffled laughter and shuffled purposefully over to the trunk.

The soft downward glow of the orb accentuated the hunch of his shoulders, the folds of his cape and the weaving action of his hands as he turned to address them.

'Ladies and gentlemen! Tonight, for the first time ever, I will endeavour to move two bodies through space simultaneously.'

He stooped to open the lid of the trunk.

'At the very same time Mr Warren is travelling through the unknown to arrive here, I will transport myself from this chest to the box where he is now.'

A ripple of anticipation moved through the small crowd.

'But,' he lowered his voice for effect, 'for an instant in time, we will be as one, our atoms joined in that mystical, marvellous, magical dimension that separates and unites us all.'

They fell silent. Even Brad stopped laughing inside his box.

The orb began to pulse.

Mahmoud climbed into the trunk and carefully, painfully, folded his twisted frame into it.

The heavy lid fell shut with a dull thud.

In that instant, the pulsing of the orb began to increase in intensity until it became impossible to look at.

All at once the night was filled with the sound of children laughing. The sound came from above them, behind them, beside them — all around. And there was another sound — singing. A boy's voice, sad and alone. So alone.

Then Kate remembered. The crippled Indian boy whose parents owned the fruit shop across the road from her school bus stop so many years ago. There were all kinds of stories about that boy: that he had the face of a dog, hair all over his body, and the hands of an amphibian; that he had to take correspondence lessons because he was too malformed to go to school with normal children. For a long time he was little more than the subject of malevolent rumour. Out of sight, but not out of mind. Then one day, when she was about twelve years old, she heard beautiful singing as she passed the fruit shop early one morning. It was the same lonely voice she could hear now. She'd stopped and looked in. There, at the back of the shop, singing to himself while he carefully arranged oranges on a low display tray, was the boy she'd heard so much about. Not at all like the monster she had imagined, just a small, helpless, hunched boy in a wheelchair. She found herself walking into the shop in the hope of talking to him. But, alerted by the click of her shoes on the tiled floor, he had turned, seen her and wheeled quickly away through a door screened by dangling plastic strips.

She didn't go after him.

In the years that followed, she'd seen him quite often, watching from an upstairs window while she laughed and flirted at the bus stop. She remembered wondering how he got up those stairs. And even from that distance she remembered seeing — or was it feeling? — pain in his eyes and thinking it must be physical. It never occurred to her that it might be the pain of longing for something he could never have.

Despite the teasing of her friends she'd often smile and wave at him, but he would just melt back into the anonymity of his room without returning the gesture.

The uncanny thing was, even though she had never been close enough to notice such details, she seemed to recall clearly that the little boy had emerald-green eyes — just like Mahmoud's.

Suddenly, it was over. The orb ceased to pulse. The night was silent.

With a quiet creak the trunk lid began to lift. Slowly, shakily, Brad emerged, checking himself all over as if to make sure that he was all there.

He looked across to the box he'd been shut into on the side of the stage and shook his head in amazement.

'All done with mirrors, eh, Brad?' Tammy Anderson teased.

Brad just smiled self-consciously.

There was no sign of Mahmoud.

'Where's the magician?' someone asked.

'Show yourself, Mahmoud,' another cried. 'Look in the Dr. Who phone booth thingy, Brad, see if he's in there!'

But Brad didn't appear to want any further part in the proceedings. He stepped down off the stage and made his way towards Kate.

Urged on by the others, Tammy climbed onto the stage to investigate. She opened the door of the phone booth-like box but he wasn't there.

Others climbed up and began to search the stage for trapdoors or secret compartments. There was none.

'I bet he's in the truck,' someone suggested and went to check.

He wasn't there, either.

By now, Brad was holding Kate in a fierce embrace. 'I'm sorry,' he whispered. 'I'm so sorry.'

'It's all right,' she said.

'I always loved you, only I—'

'I know.'

He began to cry.

Even as she held him, Kate knew that the bitterness had gone from Brad. This had been the magician's gift to her, the gift of a boy who had loved her from afar. He had shown her that before magic can be real you have to believe in it. He'd put the magic back into her marriage and given her another chance at happiness. She wanted to thank him for that. She wanted to tell him she remembered who he was. She wanted to talk to him about so many things. But she never got the chance because he didn't reappear that evening.

And later that night when, in the middle of their lovemaking, she looked up and saw the look of compassion and deep understanding in Brad's emerald-green eyes, she understood why Mahmoud the Magnificent would never be seen again.

GROWING OLD WITH RICHARD

The narrow road twisted like a pretzel through the heavily wooded valley. Even on a dry day the deceptive bends had to be negotiated carefully; on a night like tonight — with a cyclone lashing in from the northeast — the going was treacherous.

The driver of the Jaguar travelled this same stretch of road every day, but for all he could see in tonight's conditions he might as well have been blindfolded. The Jag's headlights groped valiantly through the downpour, the bright beams bouncing off saturated tree trunks, tangled lantana, angry little waterfalls and a luminous yellow sign that warned that the road was slippery when wet.

The driver noticed none of this — he had other things

on his mind. Despite the conditions, he drove as if pursued by the devil.

Down near the bottom of the valley, what was usually a small spring-fed stream that trickled tamely through a drain under the road had swollen into a raging torrent that spewed menacingly out across the bitumen on the elbow of a sharp bend. At the speed it was travelling, the Jaguar had no chance: its rear end drifted, the driver overcorrected, the car began to roll.

For a few sickening seconds the valley was filled with the sound of tortured metal and breaking glass. Then there was only the relentless hammering of the rain and the muffled moans of a dying man.

Astrid turned away from the window. *God, what an awful night!* She checked her watch. Richard said he had a few house calls to make after golf and he'd be back by six thirty — it was now ten past seven. She shook her head and smiled a long-suffering smile — running late seemed to be an occupational habit with her husband. If anything, he was getting worse. He never seemed to get anywhere on time these days, especially in the evenings. She'd lost count of how many dinner parties they'd arrived at late, flustered and apologetic; or how many cinemas they'd stumbled into ten minutes after the movie had commenced; and as for church ...

He was never late for golf, though; his tee-off time was sacrosanct.

Sighing with resignation, she absent-mindedly wiped her already dry hands on her apron and made her way back into the kitchen where she turned on the oven light and peered in through the eye-level glass door to check the roast. It was a huge leg of pork, far too big for just the two of them. After a lifetime of buying food for a family, she still hadn't adjusted to buying for just two. Tonight, however, her oversight had given her an ideal excuse to invite the family around for dinner. She was looking forward to that; she missed them.

For years she had looked forward to nothing so much as the day that Emma and Johnny would leave home and she and Richard would be alone again. Now that time had come, she didn't like it at all. She was unprepared for — what was it Emma called it? — her *space*. For the first time in longer than she could remember, she was free to do what she liked, when she liked. She had choices. The trouble was, she didn't know what to do with them. Her days, once so full, were now depressingly empty. She even began to pine for the tiresome, menial, child-minding tasks she had loathed for years. As much as she had moaned about them at the time, she now discovered, to her surprise, that they were the very things that let her know she was needed. Now that she no longer had to do these things for her family, she no longer felt needed. It was a stupid reaction, she knew that, and everyone assured her the feeling would pass; but Johnny had been gone three years now and Emma nearly two, and she still felt the same.

For a time, a kind of madness had come over her — she began moving furniture around for no reason; she dusted and polished until the house positively gleamed; she rearranged the bookshelves — first in alphabetical order, then by category, finally by author; she spent hours cooking banquet-like four-course meals, which she produced ceremoniously every night, until Richard begged her to stop before she killed them both.

Then, in a complete turnaround, she lapsed into lethargy, a period of sloth when she did little except consume endless cups of tea and stacks of popular romance novels. The garden and the house fell into disarray and takeaway meals became the norm rather than the exception. She even developed a mild addiction to daytime television.

Eventually, recognising — with not a little horror — that soap operas now offered more entertainment than her own life, she decided that something had to be done. But what? The children had given her focus; they were her work, her hobby, her passion. Even now whenever she walked past their bedrooms she half expected to find Johnny strewn across his bed like the aftermath of a hurricane, or Emma — neat and tidy Emma — seated at her desk looking out over the garden and tapping away happily at her computer. But those days were gone. For ever. Her children had claimed their independence and in doing so given back hers. But this newfound freedom terrified her. She felt as though she had been abandoned in a wide-open unfamiliar space with no fences, no boundaries, no roads, no maps — only endless horizons and limitless possibilities.

She had never felt so alone.

'Alone, nonsense, what am I, Scotch mist?' Richard said as he bent intently over the putt he was lining up on the living room carpet.

'You know what I mean.'

'Do I?' he said, as the ball rolled towards the little machine that would return it to him if his putt found its mark.

'Over twenty years, Rick, and now ...'

'Peace and quiet!' Richard said and grunted triumphantly as the ball popped back towards him.

'I don't think I'm cut out for so much peace and quiet.'

'You'll get used to it. You'll find plenty to do.'

She made no reply.

He came and sat on the arm of the couch beside her and began tapping the side of his worn carpet slipper with the putter.

She sighed. 'It's okay for you, you've got your work. And your golf.'

'Perhaps you should join a club. What about bowls?'

'Don't be silly. I'm not *that* old.'

'Lots of people play bowls, not just old people. You never know, you might like it.'

'I might, but that's not the point. I need more than that. I can't spend the rest of my life playing bowls.' She swivelled slightly to face him. 'Perhaps I should get a job.'

'What on earth for? We don't need the money.'

'It's not about the money.'

Richard prided himself on being a modern man: he was, for instance, an active and vocal supporter of equal pay for women long before it became fashionable; however, in his heart, he far preferred having Astrid at home doing the wife and mother things that seemed so wrong to many, yet so right to him. It was undeniably a sexist attitude, but one he was perfectly comfortable with. Whereas, the thought of coming home to an empty house and having to prepare meals and do his own washing and cleaning, while Astrid went in pursuit of a career, gave him no comfort at all.

'What kind of job?' he asked.

'I don't know. Anything. I'm not looking for a career — it's a bit late for that — just something to beat the boredom.'

'A lot of jobs *are* boring.'

'Well, I can't mope around here and prune roses for the rest of my life. I'll go batty.'

The tone in her voice told him that the matter required serious consideration, but it was too large a subject to deal with at this late hour. He decided to sleep on it and to try to make some worthwhile suggestions in the morning. With any luck she would have forgotten about it by then.

'You'll be all right, you'll think of something, you'll see,' he said kissing her fondly on the top of the head.

With that he went back to his putting machine, leaving her to gaze wistfully at the empty armchair that used to be Johnny's favourite.

Astrid turned the potatoes and closed the oven door; Carlos would make his famous gravy later — he could cook anything, that boy.

Richard had been furious when Emma first told them she was going to live with Carlos. He'd never denied his daughter anything, but when he discovered that she was going to live — in sin — with a penniless Filipino law student, he had protested vehemently. There was nothing racial in this, simply a father's natural reluctance to accept that his daughter could give herself so completely to any man — let alone one who was far too good-looking to be trusted.

On the other hand, Richard hadn't said a thing when Johnny had moved in with Sarah, a woman who was nearly ten years older than him.

It was Astrid who'd been upset about this.

In the end there was nothing they could do about either relationship. Sometimes, the best way to hold on to your children is to let them go, and as hard as it had been, that's what they had done.

In time, they had become reasonably accustomed to

their de facto in-laws; in fact, Carlos had quite endeared himself to them.

Astrid still had her doubts about Sarah, though.

They were all coming for dinner tonight. With any luck they would stay the night. Lord knows there was enough room. The house was far too big for two. They talked about moving, getting something smaller, an apartment or a townhouse, but the family home was filled with fond memories, and Astrid had developed a deep and meaningful relationship with every tree and shrub in the garden. Besides, there were the future grandchildren to consider — they would need a big house when they came to stay.

She smiled to herself as she made her way into the living room. It seemed like only yesterday that she had been falling madly, irresponsibly in love with a lanky medical student named Richard Howarth; now, here she was, wrapped warmly in a boring woollen cardigan, kneeling carefully on her less than flexible knees, stoking the fire and dreaming about the visits of her as yet unborn grandchildren.

She found a long grey hair on the hearth and tossed it into the fire; hers or Richard's? It was getting hard to tell.

Suddenly, a flash of lightning lit up the room. A deafening crack of thunder followed seconds later. The centre of the storm was moving closer. She shivered, threw another piece of wood on the fire and rocked back to sit on the rug and stare vacantly into the flames.

———

She worried about Richard driving in the rain — he was getting so inattentive in his old age. Lately, she'd noticed a few dents and scratches in the Jag, which he hadn't said anything about. Then again, he wouldn't — he was very proud of his driving record. 'Forty years and not one prang!' he'd boast proudly, especially to Johnny, who at twenty-two had already had two accidents in his Kombi — although, to be fair, one wasn't his fault.

There was another loud crack in the heavens and the house was plunged into blackness. *Damn!*

Luckily, she was cooking with gas; the dinner wouldn't be ruined.

When her eyes grew accustomed to the darkness, she went in search of candles.

The traffic was backed up for half a mile either side of the accident. As always, a gang of tow trucks had arrived out of nowhere, like vultures ready to fight to the death over the metallic carrion. Tonight they would feast. There had already been a secondary five-car pile-up involving the first few cars that had tried to avoid the Jag lying on its back in the middle of the road. The conditions made sudden braking impossible. More accidents were inevitable. The tow truck drivers were literally licking their lips.

The police weren't so happy. Handling a situation like this was difficult at any time; on a night like this, it was hell. Thankfully, no one had been seriously hurt in the secondary accidents, so there was no need to call in more than one ambulance. The driver of the Jag hadn't been so lucky.

One of the policemen held the licence he'd found in the dead driver's wallet. He hated this part of the job. He read the details over the car radio. Let some other poor bastard break the news to the family; he was going to be up half the night trying to sort out the chaos. What a shit of a night to die.

'No one's home,' said Emma in dismay as they pulled up outside the house.

'No, it's just a power failure,' Carlos said.

'How can you tell?'

'The streetlights are out.'

'Lightning, probably,' said Johnny.

'There's Astrid.' Sarah pointed at the torch-bearing shape walking down the front path towards them.

Astrid was hunched under an umbrella and as she got closer they could see she was carrying two more.

Trust Mum to have spare umbrellas, Emma thought as she leapt out of the car and splashed up the path to embrace her mother.

'Silly girl, you'll get soaked!' Astrid chided.

'Oh, stop panicking,' Emma said as she planted a kiss on her mother's forehead. She was a lot taller than Astrid, more like her father — only in height, thankfully; she hadn't inherited the bumbling, awkward mannerisms that were adorable in Richard but would have been quite unfortunate in a young lady.

Emma took one of the umbrellas, opened it, and made her way back to the car. Astrid followed.

'Where's the Kombi?' Astrid asked when she saw Johnny and Sarah in the car — she had to speak loudly to be heard over the hammering of the rain on the umbrellas.

'Service station,' Emma shouted.

'Not another accident?'

'Give me a break, Mum,' Johnny said as he got out of the car, took the other umbrella, and held it over the door as Sarah climbed out. 'I'm having a head gasket replaced, that's all.'

'Oh, that's all right then,' Astrid smiled, seeming happier even though she had no idea what a head gasket was. 'Hello, Sarah, how are you?' she said as Sarah joined them.

'Fine, thank you.'

'Good to see you, dear,' Astrid said and kissed her quickly on the cheek. It was a polite greeting, but not exactly warm. Astrid still couldn't understand why a thirty-eight-year-old woman would choose to live with a boy nearly twelve years her junior. The only possible reason she could think of made her very uncomfortable. 'Come along, let's get you all inside before you catch your death,' she said adopting a mother's tone.

'Yes, Mommy,' teased Carlos, who was now sharing an umbrella with Emma. He had an intriguing accent, sort of

American-Asian. All Filipinos spoke this way, he'd told them, largely the result of the American television shows they grow up with — God help them.

While she may have had reservations about Sarah, Astrid openly adored Carlos. She often found herself thinking what beautiful children he and Emma would have. She was definitely warming to the whole idea of being a grandparent — although it was rather premature; there had been no mention of marriage from either couple, let alone children. Still, one could always dream.

'Where's Dad?' Johnny asked when they were in the candlelit living room drying themselves before the fire.

'He had a few house calls to make after golf,' Astrid explained. 'I expected him home around six thirty. But, you know your father, once he gets involved in something, he tends to lose track of time.'

'Maybe he tried to call,' Emma suggested.

'Is the phone working?' Carlos asked.

'I never thought to check,' Astrid said. 'Wouldn't it be out because of the power failure?'

'Not necessarily, unless the lightning struck a pole nearby, or something like that.'

'I heard it wasn't a good idea to use a telephone during a thunderstorm,' Sarah said. 'I'm not sure why.'

'But if your father can't get through ...' Astrid worried.

'I'll check,' Johnny grunted. He was back within seconds. 'Dead as a dodo.'

'There, that it explains it,' Emma said.

'I wish he'd use his mobile,' Astrid said to no one in particular. 'I don't even know why he bothers having one, he never turns it on.'

'It's his little rebellion,' Emma said. 'Says he did just fine for years without one and can't see why it's necessary now.'

'The last of the Luddites,' Johnny laughed.

'Lud whats?' Sarah asked.

While Johnny expounded on the little he knew about Luddites, Astrid's gaze strayed to a recent photograph of Richard that sat on the china cabinet among all the other gilt-framed memories. Even though the wear and tear of the years had etched creases into his face, she could still see the handsome, loose-limbed youth who had changed her life. Now he was as much a part of her as she was of him, and she knew that without him she would be less than whole. A chill passed through her. She gathered the cardigan tighter around her shoulders.

'I hope they get the phones fixed soon,' she said softly. 'Your father will worry if his patients can't get through.'

Emma and Johnny looked at each other and smiled — they knew it wasn't the patients their mother was worried about.

'I'm sure they'll have the phones fixed in no time,' Emma assured her.

'No worries,' Johnny agreed.

Eventually, at Astrid's insistence, they ate without Richard. Carlos wanted to go and look for him but Astrid talked him out of it. She didn't know where to tell him to start looking. 'A few house calls' was all Richard had said. He never said with whom — he never did.

Later, when the last of the apple pie had been demolished and there was still no word from him, they were all beginning to worry openly.

He was now nearly three hours overdue.

'Perhaps we should check the hospitals,' Emma suggested.

'Don't even *say* that!' Astrid said sharply.

'I mean, maybe there was an emergency and he had to take one of his patients there,' Emma explained, quickly.

Astrid was embarrassed by her own over-reaction. 'Oh, sorry, how stupid of me. I'm fairly sure he'd be at North Shore if that were the case.'

'Maybe I should go and check?' Carlos offered, not really relishing the thought of such a mission in the atrocious conditions.

'No, if he's had to go to the hospital, it would have to be something really important and he wouldn't want to be disturbed. I honestly don't think we should worry. He's been late before — there's always a good reason,' Astrid said bravely.

'Yes, but three hours ...' Emma said.

Hearing the dangerously contagious sound of panic in his sister's voice, Johnny cut in quickly. 'I'm sure you're right, Mum, he'll be caught up in something important.'

A car came hissing slowly down the sodden street. Astrid got up quickly, went to the window and drew back the curtains. Her shoulders slumped as the car drove on by. She continued staring out at the relentless downpour — if anything, it was heavier now.

'C'mon, Johnny, let's you and I do the dishes,' Sarah said, in an effort to change the subject.

Astrid turned from the window. 'No, leave them. I'll put them in the dishwasher.'

'Nonsense, there's no power, remember?' Sarah said, rising to her feet. 'You sit down and relax. We'll do the dishes and make coff—'

'I said *leave them!*'

Sarah sat back down, plainly shocked.

Emma went to her mother. 'Mum?'

Astrid turned to Sarah. 'I'm sorry, I ...'

'It's all right,' Sarah said, drily.

Astrid went across to her. 'Sarah ...'

'It's all right, really,' Sarah said, but continued to stare stonily at her empty plate.

Johnny's heart went out to them; he understood what was happening, but it was something they had to work out for themselves.

Astrid put a comforting hand on Sarah's shoulder. 'Come on, I'll help you make coffee. We'll let the others go and laze around the fire.'

'Top idea,' Johnny agreed and bolted from the room before the idea of him doing the dishes raised its ugly head again.

Carlos and Emma followed discreetly.

———

For a while Sarah and Astrid managed to avoid each other in the large kitchen. Astrid kept busy stacking things in the lifeless dishwasher, while Sarah put a pot of water on the stove and ground coffee beans.

Soon the kitchen was tidy and there was nothing for them to do but sit and wait for the water to boil.

Sarah sat on one side of the kitchen table fiddling with the cups she had stacked on a tray along with milk, sugar and a plate of after-dinner mints.

Astrid sat opposite, studying her.

Sarah was a fine-looking woman with high cheekbones, intelligent hazel eyes, and thick, dark, shoulder-length hair framing an attractive, open face. She wore little make-up — just a hint around the eyes and a touch of lipstick. Her beauty was natural, she would age well — not that she was any spring chicken now. And perhaps because of her age there was an air of maturity about her — a confidence. Perhaps it was her confidence that Astrid found so threatening. Here was a woman who was more than capable of looking after her son, and there was no doubt he needed looking after. But why would any woman choose to live with a boy so much younger than her in every way? Why didn't she have a man more her own age? *What was wrong with her?*

Sarah spoke first. 'You're worried about him, aren't you?'

'Richard? Yes, of course I am.'

'No ... well ... yes, of course you're worried about

Richard. What I meant was … you're worried about Johnny, aren't you?'

'Not really, it's just …'

'I love him, you know.'

'Are you sure?'

'I'm sure.'

'Have you ever actually *thought* about what you're doing?'

'Of course I have.'

'Well, I can't see why—'

'You don't see why a woman my age would want to get involved with someone so much younger.'

'Exactly. If you want to know the truth, I think it's irresponsible.'

'And futile?'

'That, too.'

Sarah sighed. It wasn't easy explaining what she felt — even to herself. Usually she didn't try, but this was Johnny's mother. 'Do you have any idea what kind of pressure people put on a woman my age who doesn't even have a steady boyfriend, let alone a husband?'

'You're not going to tell me you're with Johnny because of the pressure other people put on you?' Astrid said aghast.

'On the contrary, what they thought didn't bother me at all. I'd simply explain, truthfully, that staying unattached was my choice, that there were things I wanted to do, places I had to see, and long-term commitments, particularly marriage, just didn't fit into my plans.'

'What about children?'

'You see — you're doing it, too. That's exactly what people always say. They just can't seem to accept that a woman might not want a family. It's okay for a man to want to be footloose and family free, but if a woman chooses to do that, she's considered to be some kind of freak.'

'You don't want children?'

'I didn't say that.'

'Well — do you?'

'I don't know.'

'What do you mean, *you don't know?*'

'Sometimes I do, sometimes I don't. I'm just not sure, that's all. And I want to be very sure.'

'You'd better make up your mind soon.'

'I don't need you to tell me that.'

'No, I'm sorry, I didn't mean to ... it's just that Johnny's so young—'

'And soon I'll be too old?'

Astrid looked down at her hands. 'It's possible. There are risks ...'

'Yes, I know, that's something I'll have to deal with if it ever arises.'

'*If?*'

'Yes, *if.*' Sarah waited for Astrid to look up at her. When she resumed, her voice was softer, almost sad. 'You're assuming too much, Astrid. You think I'm in control of all this, but I'm not. I love Johnny, that's all. It's good old-fashioned, uncomplicated, irrational love. Stupid, I know, and often embarrassing as well, but it's love for all that. The problem is, I'm not sure it will be enough.'

'I don't understand ...'

'I'm not sure that it will be enough for marriage, babies, a lifetime together. Do you really think you're the only one who worries about our age difference? Hell, I live with it every day.'

'Johnny says he loves you.'

'Of course he says he loves me — and he does ... for now. But as you're well aware, he's only a boy. You and I know that things can change over time. Stuff happens. Who knows where we'll be in a few years' time? When he's thirty-five, I'll be nearly fifty — nature's not all that kind to fifty-year-old women. Even now my body's not what it used to be — my tits are already beginning to sag a bit.'

'Too much information.'

'Why? Sex is what it's all about, isn't it? Be honest, you think I seduced Johnny, don't you? A shameless old cougar having her last fling with a bit of young stuff.'

'Certainly not. I've never thought anything of the kind.'

'Tell the truth, Astrid.'

Astrid's blush betrayed her.

'Don't be embarrassed,' Sarah said. 'I admit sex is part of it — it wouldn't be much of a relationship without it, would it? But there's a lot more to it than that. For the first time in my life I know what 'in sickness and in health, for richer, for poorer' and all that stuff really means. It's how I feel when I'm with Johnny. And it's *wonderful*. And do you know what's the best thing? He makes me laugh. Sounds silly, I know, but he can always make me laugh and that's a big part of what we have.'

Astrid smiled knowingly.

'Everyone tells me it can't last,' Sarah continued. 'And I'm sure they're right. I don't think Johnny's ever going to ask me to marry him. To be perfectly honest, I'm not even sure I'd accept if he did. I'm not certain it would be the right thing for either of us. But, right now, I'm the happiest I've ever been in my life. It may be the only chance I'll ever have to be this happy. So I'm going to hold on to it for as long as I can. When it's over, it will be over, but it will *never* be wrong.'

Astrid understood — Sarah was right, it's important to make the most of the happy times, God knows they can be all too short. She tried to imagine life without Richard — life without laughter — she couldn't. They had been lucky their love had endured where many had failed. The original heat of their youthful passion may have gone, but in its place had grown a respect, a certainty — a good, honest, compassionate love. They had never had to suffer the mind-sapping deceit and bitterness that had savaged the marriages of so many of their friends. The only threat stalking them was the unrelenting march of time. And even with that, there was the comfort of knowing you had someone to grow old with. She was growing old with Richard and on the whole the prospect didn't seem too awful.

For the first time in a very long time she didn't feel confused, alone or unwanted. She wanted to tell Richard. He would understand and he would be glad. But where on earth was he?

She reached out and took Sarah's hand for the comfort it gave them both. The water boiled unnoticed.

A police car crawled slowly down the street, a torch beam probing out of the passenger window searching for street numbers in the impossible light. It was amazing how few homes had their street numbers displayed; frustrating as hell when you were trying to find a particular address in a hurry.

As he played the torch beam over the unnumbered letterboxes, Sergeant Jim Lawrence was trying to ignore the icy lump in his stomach. He hated doing what he was about to do, but you couldn't just phone — such things had to be done in person.

The lights on the street began to flicker and houses blazed back to life all around them.

'Ah, a little light on the subject,' mumbled Jurd, the pudding-faced constable who was driving.

A quick glance at the few letterbox numbers they could see told them they were at the wrong end of the street but were headed in the right direction. They continued driving at the same deliberate speed; they were in no hurry.

Eventually, they stopped in front of a large Federation-style home that glowed invitingly through the downpour.

'Bloody millionaires,' Jurd said, eyeing the house enviously.

'Not exactly on the breadline, that's for sure,' Sergeant Lawrence agreed. He could never afford a place like this, but he was happy enough with his humble abode. Besides, a huge home and money in the bank is no guarantee of happiness. Appearances can be very deceiving. What you see isn't necessarily what you get. Tonight was another case in point. Jesus, he hated having to wade through the crap of other people's lives.

He noticed a middle-aged woman looking anxiously out of the window, probably the wife. He saw her hunch over as she recognised the police car. Someone put his or her arms around her. Sergeant Lawrence silently thanked God she had somebody with her. It was going to be hard enough breaking the news of the doctor's death; how on earth was he going to tell them about the other body in the back seat — the bruised and naked little girl, with her thin helpless hands bound together by surgical tape?

Astrid sold the house, moved to the Gold Coast and joined a bowling club. Johnny swears he will quit drinking by Christmas. If he does, there's a chance Sarah will come back to him. Emma married Carlos and they are very much in love. They have a son. They did not name him Richard.

53

The fat man's breath rattled savagely in his throat as he watched the Jaguar slide to a halt and the girl scramble sobbing into it. He smashed his fist into the trunk of the tree that hid him from the road. The bitch! If he hadn't slipped over in the mud she would never have escaped. He cursed aloud as the car's tail-lights were swallowed by the darkness. He pulled the roll of surgical tape from his pocket and hurled it away in fury. His hand hurt. Looking down, he saw that it was bleeding. Despite the cold he was sweating freely. He wiped the torn dress across his forehead and smelled the scent of her. It filled his head with pictures of lacy-edged sheets, fluffy pillows and little white flowers on pink wallpaper. He thought of his mother. He was late for his dinner and covered in mud — she would be furious. He hated to make Mummy angry. He would need to think of a really good excuse.

YIN AND YANG

Simon and Jenny Collins are an unlikely couple. Were you to meet them individually you'd never guess she could possibly be married to him, or vice versa. As it happens, however, they are very much in love — a classic case of opposites attracting.

They met at a party hosted by one of Simon's clients.

After arriving late and enquiring after Charles, his host, Simon was handed a glass of champagne by a rent-a-waiter and directed through some French doors towards a group of people standing on the far side of the swimming pool. As casually as you can when you're at a party where everyone knows everyone but you, he made his way around to join the happy group.

Drawing near, he saw they were gathered around an

animated dark-haired woman who appeared to be regaling them with some tale they obviously found amusing.

Charles, who was standing next to the woman and laughing loudest, spied Simon approaching. 'Simon, old boy, I was beginning to wonder where you'd got to.'

Simon hesitated.

'Come on, man, don't stand there on your lonesome. Come and meet Jenny!' Charles said as he placed an enthusiastic hand on the shoulder of the woman by his side.

She, like everyone else, looked at Simon. Her smile was warm.

The others parted slightly to let him through.

Jenny extended a slender tanned hand to him. 'Pleased to meet you, Simon,' she said in a way that told him she meant it.

'Likewise,' he replied, feeling like an intruder.

The others were introduced in turn and although he made a genuine effort to memorise their features for future reference, it was Jenny's face that lingered clearest in his mind. A radiantly healthy face, with honey-coloured eyes that seemed brightened by an inner light.

Maybe she's a vegetarian, he thought, for no rational reason, and, being omnivorous himself, found this concerned him. He wondered why.

Charles interrupted his thoughts.

'Known Jenny since school,' he was saying. 'All us chaps chased her back then. Waste of time, though — she wasn't interested in any of us. Perhaps you'll have better luck,' he added, tactlessly, as his wife, Heather, arrived to tell them dinner was ready.

Simon and Jenny, each embarrassed in their own way by Charles's introduction, were visibly relieved by Heather's timely announcement.

Jenny fell in by his side as they drifted in for dinner. 'Charles is a bit over the top sometimes,' she said.

'Means well, I'm sure,' Simon said, nervously.

She felt his discomfort. 'You look a bit lost,' she said.

'Well, to tell the truth, I don't know a soul here other than Charles, and we only met recently.'

'At work or play?'

'He's a client.'

'And you're ...?'

'A solicitor.'

'Well, Simon solicitor, stick by me and I'll give you the lowdown on everyone here; all their dark secrets,' she promised mischievously.

An evening of gossip was not normally a prospect he would have looked forward to, but if it meant staying close to this captivating woman in the tantalizingly-cut red dress, Simon was happy to accept.

As it happened, she didn't gossip at all. Instead, she spent most of the evening trying to get him to tell her more about himself. And whenever he lowered his guard enough to let her into some private episode in his life, she gave him her full attention.

She was as good at listening as she was at talking, which was no mean feat. It wasn't simply that she was an extrovert; it was more that she just enjoyed life. She revelled in it. And she appeared to have experienced the best and the worst of it with equal enthusiasm.

During the course of the evening she managed to cast her spell over them all but none more than Simon. He never left her side.

Being naturally shy, he found she was his perfect foil — a one-woman introduction service. By the end of that night he'd met everyone at the party and — mainly because he was with her — they'd welcomed him into their midst as they would an old friend. Although, few could fathom why Jenny should be devoting so much attention to this rather uninspiring stranger. Simon was conscious of this as well and more than a little flattered. However, he was certain Jenny's actions were motivated by good manners rather than any attraction she might have felt for him.

The truth was that not even his closest friends would have described Simon Collins as a prize catch.

Not that he was unpleasant to look at, on the contrary: he was tall and angular with vaguely aristocratic features and searching grey eyes. His smile, though at times inhibited by shyness, was warm and genuine. He was also heterosexual and reasonably well off financially; so in terms of these narrow criteria he was what one would describe as a relatively attractive eligible bachelor.

The problem was that he had such an economy of speech and lack of flair that he was, to many, a bit, well ... boring. A safe, sober, thoroughly predictable chap who had attended the same school and was now a member of the same law firm and golf club as his father. And no one, least of all Simon, would have been the slightest bit surprised if he eventually married someone his mother recommended. Neither did he feel inclined to break this mould. He was perfectly happy with his lot. He was not by nature an adventurer; he had no desire to explore life's many possibilities, nor — heaven forbid — its temptations. He had never even felt the need to travel. While most of his contemporaries were picking up a crash course in the ways of the world during postgraduate meanderings through Europe, Asia or other more exotic locations, Simon had been content to remain in Sydney getting established in the firm and making an early start in the property market. Safe, sober, reliable and totally innocuous — that was Simon Collins.

Jennifer Goddard, on the other hand, was anything but boring. She very definitely had flair. She was a traveller who had been on the move since leaving school, bypassing tertiary education for the greater training ground of planet Earth. Initially, she paid her way working as a waitress or pulling pints behind bars. Eventually, though, she began to concentrate on her talent as a commercial artist and after some very hungry months in London, was able to get enough work to get by on.

Now, ten years on, she was back in Sydney visiting family and friends and deciding whether to stay or move on again.

'Do you travel much?' she asked Simon, after giving him a brief but enthusiastic description of her recent trek through the mountains of Morocco on horseback.

'Did once — to Bali. An end-of-season rugby trip,' he said. 'Bit of a boys' bash, you know. Interesting place, I suppose, but a bit too hot and crowded for me. Got dysentery. Nearly died.' It was clear from his tone that he was not inclined to tempt fate in this way again.

Given their differences in interests and personalities, no one would have dreamt that Simon Collins could ever woo and win a prize like Jennifer Goddard. Nevertheless, that is exactly what he did.

After that first evening, he couldn't get her out of his mind. She filled his every waking hour and a good many of his dreaming ones. His concentration at work began to suffer and his once gargantuan appetite dwindled to the point where he began to lose weight.

This all took place during the time of his indecision — that limbo period when he was wondering what to do about her. Infatuation was not an emotion he was familiar with and he thought — even hoped — it would pass and let him return to his normal, comfortable, predictable existence. It wasn't to be; Jenny was in his blood and she was there to stay. Furthermore, when he came to accept this, he wasn't at all unhappy about it. On the contrary, he found it filled him with a kind of heart-stopping joy. And although he was painfully slow to decide what to do about her, once he did, he discovered within himself powers of romantic cunning neither he nor anyone else suspected he possessed.

He pursued her patiently, tactfully, ever so politely, but relentlessly. Nothing and no one could distract him from his purpose. And in time, much to everyone's dismay, it became obvious that Jenny's heart was slowly being won over by this unlikely character.

It wasn't as though he underwent any dramatic personality change to carry out this miraculous seduction; outwardly he remained pretty much the same old pinstriped Simon. Jenny, however, uncovered another side to him — the humorous, gentle, genuine person who sheltered behind his shy and somewhat lugubrious exterior. What attracted her most was the hidden strength she found lurking behind his humble facade. She discovered that Simon Collins was a man of great depth and determination. His apparent humility and reluctance to force his opinions on others was simply an overdose of good manners. Privately, he harboured strong convictions and a fervent desire to see that justice was done, wrongs righted, and the disadvantaged helped to the very nth degree of the law. What's more, unlike many of his dinner party liberal colleagues, he backed up his beliefs with action — giving freely of his time to legal aid and various environmental and charitable organisations. Not that you could ever accuse him of being radical; he was simply a concerned citizen, a man of principle, a rare man.

The more Jenny got to know him, the more she grew to love him. And she came to understand it would be this way for as long as they both would live.

Two and a half years after their first meeting, Simon walked proudly down the aisle with the radiant Mrs Jennifer Collins by his side.

And on that same day, some wag in the back of the church was heard to say: 'The perfect couple — Yin and Yang.'

This is not, however, a perfect world. It is often unfair. So it was that on a dismal winter evening in the third year of their marriage, Jenny Collins had to tell her husband that — according to the opinion of the latest of two specialists — she would never bear children. She was shattered by this news and expected he would be, too. She watched his face for signs of anger, sadness or disappointment.

It was often said that Simon was at his best in tense situations, a quality that had proven an immeasurable advantage in his profession. He had never needed this attribute more. While he was naturally devastated by Jenny's revelation, he was even more concerned with the impact it would have on her. For this reason, in less time than it takes to tell, he resolved never to let her hear or see any sign of disappointment in his words or actions. Perhaps in time, if she wanted to, they could talk about adoption; for now, all that mattered was her peace of mind. As for him, just being with Jenny gave him more happiness than any man should reasonably expect from life. If having no children was the price he had to pay for this, it seemed a fair exchange.

Jenny saw no distress in his face as she gave him the bad news. All she saw was love, unquestionable and unshaken. He reached out, pulled her gently into his arms and held her while she cried.

Later that night she offered to leave him. 'It's not fair on you, Si', or your parents ... you're their only son.'

'And you're my only wife,' he said, gently kissing the top of her head as she lay in the crook of his arm staring up at the ceiling.

They lay like this for some time.

Simon broke the silence. 'We'll travel. Somewhere new each year.'

'Oh, Simon,' she teased, giving him a gentle shove, 'you hate travelling. All I've ever heard about is your infamous bout of Bali belly.'

'I know, but you love charging off to foreign places, and if you were with me, perhaps I would, too.'

She knew he was only trying to cheer her up, but the prospect was genuinely attractive. 'Do you really think so?' she said.

'It's possible,' he said encouragingly. 'Let's try it and see.'

'Oh yes, let's!'

Simon did enjoy travelling with Jenny. Enormously. He

learned to see the world through her eyes and it was a wonderful place. At various times during the next four years he found himself rocking along South American railways, luxuriating in French chateaus, diving on Pacific reefs, and tramping across windswept Scottish isles. And every glorious moment of it was stored in his heart and captured, more tangibly, in a growing stack of photo albums.

In the fifth year of their newly nomadic life, they were on the island of Phuket — off the coast of Thailand — where, due to an unseasonable downpour, they had abandoned their beach-side hotel and were wandering around the town in search of suitable souvenirs to take back to their already over-cluttered home.

Along the way, Jenny was doing what she did best — making friends.

Speaking the local language was something she insisted on attempting in every country. Accordingly, armed with irresistible smile, indomitable spirit and well-worn translation book, she had charmed and amused the locals in every corner of the globe.

Which was exactly what she was doing at that moment.

Watching her working her magic on a tiny, giggling local girl, Simon found himself thinking, not for the first time, what a wonderful mother she would have been. For a single, sad instant, a shadow swept across his heart.

Jenny looked up brightly and swept his blues away. 'Oh,

look, Si — "Antiques and Artifacts",' she said, pointing at a tourist trap across the road.

Before he could respond she was splashing across the potholed road in search of the ultimate souvenir.

He went after her in a futile effort to protect their savings.

'Isn't she just gorgeous?' Jenny enthused some time later as she cradled a dusty, wooden figurine she had retrieved from one of the lower shelves at the rear of the shop.

Somewhere along the line Jenny had convinced herself that the best bargains were to be found hidden at the back of the shops where tourists wouldn't bother to look. It was a curious brand of logic, but she was so committed to it she invariably went ferreting about in the bowels of every store they went into.

On this occasion she'd been rifling about among some dusty ceramic pots when she'd emerged triumphantly clutching the wooden figure of a chubby female of indeterminate age, reclining on her left side against what appeared to be a melon of some kind. The figure's eyes were closed and her plump face wore a secret smile that was both magical and captivating. The figure was about the size of a small child, and when Jenny handed it to him, Simon found it surprisingly heavy.

Unfortunately, and I say *unfortunately* because he hated to be the bearer of bad tidings, Simon noticed a deep crack running down the back of the carving — no doubt the reason it had been relegated to the back shelves in the first place. Fully aware that the shopkeeper was hovering nearby, he pointed sternly at the flaw. 'The wood's split, Jen,' he said.

'Oh, it's nothing. It'll probably bring the price down,' she said, refusing to be deterred.

Simon was well used to dealing with his wife's impetuosity. 'Look, Jen, they probably make thousands of these things on this island. Let's scout around and see if we can find one in good condition. If we can't, and you're still keen, we'll come back and see if we can get this one at a good price, all right?'

'Oh, all right,' Jenny agreed, reluctantly. She knew he was only being sensible, but it broke her heart to put the adorable wooden figure back on the shelf. 'I come back later,' she said, in Thai, to the shopkeeper, who nodded vigorously and tried to steer them in the direction of a gold-plated Buddha, which they neither liked nor could afford.

Jenny declined politely and promised to return; the shopkeeper clearly didn't believe a word of it.

Aware of his wife's strong will and somewhat precipitous nature, Simon walked quickly out of the shop hoping she would follow before she had a chance to change her mind.

She emerged eventually, at a much slower pace.

Later that same day she found the perfect excuse to return for the little wooden figure — she found the ideal partner for it.

As Simon had guessed, there was an abundance of carved wooden figures like the first. They were made in pairs — male and female. The female always reclined to the left, the male to the right. Both wore the same serene look and slept peacefully against melons. Apparently, they were traditional carvings of some sort. Some were painted while others were stained. Jenny preferred the stained versions. However, while there may have been hundreds of them, each was distinctive in its own way — the type of wood, the grain, the hand of the carver, or just subtle differences in the curve of their smiles. Little things in themselves, but such was the personality of these figures — to use the term in its broadest sense — that these little differences made a big difference to the way you felt about them.

And it just so happened that the unmatched male figure Jenny found was exactly the same size and carved in the same wood as the lonely lady they had abandoned earlier. Naturally, she was convinced they were made for each other and it was her duty to bring them together. Leaving Simon with strict orders to buy the male, she hurried back to the first shop to rescue the little lady.

Somewhat bewildered by his wife's apparent obsession, Simon took a moment to study the little wooden figure in his arms. At first he had thought it was simply the soft lines and chubby cuteness of the carving that appealed to Jenny and to some extent himself, but it was more than that — the serene secret smile on the little fellow's sleeping face filled him with an inexplicable sense of calm and wellbeing. He liked that feeling.

Jenny was ecstatic. That night in the hotel she placed the two podgy wooden characters next to each other on the dressing table, polished them lovingly, and promised them each a new coat of varnish as soon as they got back to Sydney. And, never one to forget her manners, she formally introduced them to each other.

'Yin,' she said to the female, 'meet Yang!'

There was great humour amongst their friends when the news got around that Simon and Jenny had brought two funny little wooden carvings back from Thailand and called them Yin and Yang.

Finally, Jenny's agent, Phillip Dawkins, the fellow who'd uttered the infamous 'Yin and Yang' remark at the wedding, was forced to confess.

As you would expect, they accepted the joke in good spirit and henceforth, to avoid confusion, the little wooden figures — who now occupied pride of place on the mantelpiece in their lounge — became known as little Yin and little Yang.

The following year was the best Simon had ever experienced in the practice. Not so much that it was more profitable, which it was, but more that it was so easy. What began as acrimonious litigations quickly developed into benign out-of-court settlements; the most complex contracts were drawn up without a hiccup; and even a couple of divorce cases that had all the signs of being protracted and messy somehow worked themselves out so amicably he began to wonder why the couples were getting divorced at all. It was as though everyone he dealt with had, by some tacit arrangement, agreed to make life easy for him.

Jenny had a remarkable year as well. Not only did she get more interesting and challenging commissions, she also found her work improved dramatically. It was inspired. So much so that during the course of that year she picked up a couple of international commercial illustration awards and her agent, Phillip, was so impressed, that — in an uncharacteristic display of generosity — he offered to sponsor an exhibition for her. That, too, was a raging success.

It was during this time that they both, independently, came to the conclusion that their good fortune was somehow due to the presence of little Yin and little Yang. They never discussed this with each other — for fear of being teased — but whenever either of them was alone with the little wooden figurines, they'd find themselves talking to them as if they were speaking to real people. So it was that, during the course of that year, little Yin and little Yang came to share all the successes, secrets and dreams of Simon and Jenny Collins.

Then, amazingly, Jenny fell pregnant.

Her doctor was astounded. 'It's a bloody miracle' was all he could say.

Simon and Jenny didn't care how it happened; there is no point in trying to rationalise miracles.

'But how?' people would ask.

'Oh, just a little Yin and Yang,' they would reply, and that seemed as good an explanation as any.

Their daughter, Rebecca, arrived whole, healthy and right on time. Where some babies cry constantly and never sleep, Rebecca chuckled when awake, slept soundly when she was supposed to, woke at a civilised hour and — just like her mother — charmed everyone she met. She was a happy and contented baby with the proudest parents in the world.

About six months after Rebecca was born, Jenny discovered that Simon, too, was in the habit of talking to little Yin and little Yang.

She awoke one humid moonlit night to find him gone from their bed, and when after ten minutes he hadn't returned, she began to worry something might be wrong with Rebecca.

She climbed out of bed to investigate.

As soon as she reached the hall and heard Simon's calm voice and Rebecca's happy gurgling coming from the living room she relaxed — whatever the problem had been, Simon obviously had it under control.

She smiled at the thought of the funny serious expression he always wore when talking to his tiny daughter and tiptoed down the hall to spy on them.

However, when she peeked into the living room she

saw that although Simon was cradling and rocking his daughter in his arms, he was actually talking to little Yin and little Yang. There could be no doubt about it.

Furthermore, at one point he even appeared to hold Rebecca up so that little Yin and Yang could get a better look at her.

Strangely, Jenny was a bit uncomfortable with this. It seemed wrong for Simon to be acting this way. While it may have been acceptable for her to talk to wooden carvings — being artistic she could be forgiven a little lunacy — Simon was always so rational; it was one of the things she had come to rely on. To see him talking to inanimate objects was disorientating. It unsettled her. She went to walk away but as she shifted her weight, a floorboard creaked.

Simon looked around. 'Jenny?'

'Did she wake you?' Jenny whispered as she entered the room. Rebecca began chuckling even more enthusiastically upon hearing her mother approach.

'Yes, the little monkey, she needed a change. She'll go back to sleep without any trouble,' Simon replied as he handed Rebecca to her.

'She always does, she's a booodiful liddle lady,' Jenny cooed.

Simon looked ill at ease and vulnerable.

'I saw you talking to them, you know,' Jenny said without looking up.

'Talking to who?'

'You know ...'

'I wasn't, I was just ...'

'Don't worry, I do, too.'

'Really?' Simon said arching his eyebrows. He wasn't sure whether she was just saying this to make him feel better — that was the sort of thing she would do.

'Often,' she assured him.

They stared silently at the serene little figures. Rebecca was breathing softly and evenly on the verge of sleep.

'Sometimes I could swear they're listening,' Simon said.

Jenny couldn't help wondering what his friends would think if they knew that dear old stuffy Simon found comfort in talking to wooden figures and, furthermore, believed they might be listening to him.

'Although, I have to admit,' Simon went on, 'they don't say much.'

They laughed at this and even little Rebecca gurgled away happily as if she understood the joke.

Later, when they were back in bed wrestling with insomnia, Jenny said: 'Si, has it ever occurred to you how good things have been for us ever since little Yin and little Yang arrived?'

'You mean business-wise?'

'And Rebecca.'

'Rebecca?'

'Well, there doesn't seem to be any other explanation, does there? All the specialists were positive it was impossible for me to have children — and here we all are.'

Simon sighed.

'Let's not get too carried away, Jen. They're just a couple of wooden figures, charming and all that, but just cleverly carved teak all the same.'

'Why do you talk to them, then?'

'I don't know.'

'Probably for the same reason I do.'

'And what's that?'

'I think they want me to.'

'Really, Jen—'

'I'm serious, Si, I think it makes them happy to share in our lives. It's like ever since we brought them together, they've been part of our family. Or we've been part of theirs,' she said in a tone that was both earnest and puzzled.

'You haven't been dabbling with the dreaded weed again, have you?'

(Simon didn't forbid his wife's occasional use of marijuana, but neither did he approve; it was, after all, against the law.)

'No, I haven't,' she said indignantly. 'Anyway, you obviously feel there's something out of the ordinary about them, otherwise you wouldn't talk to them, would you?'

He tried unsuccessfully to think of an appropriate reply.

'Well, would you?' she repeated.

'Okay, I admit I do treat them like they're special. I mean they're peaceful-looking little buggers, aren't they? The way they smile ... it's like they know something we don't.'

'Mmmm ... exactly.'

'I don't want you to get the wrong idea about all this, Jennifer,' he hastened to add, a little stuffily. 'I mean, it's harmless, really, the way I talk to them. It's not as though I *pray* to them or anything like that. I just tell them things, that's all — especially good news.'

'And there's been a lot of good news for us recently, hasn't there?'

'Yes, there has. I suppose that's why I've been talking to them more often of late,' he said, happy to seize upon any rational excuse for his irrational behaviour.

'Well, you can say what you like, as far as I'm concerned there's something very special about little Yin and little Yang.'

'All I know for sure is there's something very special about big Yin,' Simon grinned as he rolled over to hug her. 'And my luck changed from the very first moment I laid eyes on you.'

'Flatterer,' Jenny teased, contentedly. 'And I suppose you're hoping you'll get lucky right now?'

'Incredible! You always know exactly what I'm thinking.'

Some weeks later, Simon's law firm held its annual end-of-year function for staff and clients. It was a black-tie affair and, if past years were anything to go by, a night not to be missed. Jenny was really looking forward to it and, although not by nature a party person, Simon was, too.

However, he wasn't at all comfortable with Jenny's choice of babysitter. 'Leigh Goodwin?! She's just a child.'

'She's fourteen, Si. Maggie uses her all the time and she's always been terrific with her kids.'

'Maggie's kids are a lot older, they hardly need looking after.'

'Just get dressed and stop whining,' Jenny said. It was far too late in the day to be having this discussion.

'Have you seen her hair?' Simon persisted, standing at the bathroom door. 'It looks like a packet of exploding jellybeans.'

'We all go through that stage,' Jenny said as she poured herself into a stunning black dress. 'I bet you had a weird hairstyle when you were her age.'

'No, I bloody well did not!' Simon said, grumpily — and he hadn't either. 'She's probably a bloody drug addict,' he muttered as he shuffled back to the bathroom mirror to fiddle unhappily with his bow tie.

'What's that, sweetheart?' Jenny said, trying not to laugh.

'Nothing,' he grumbled.

Simon was wrong, Leigh Goodwin wasn't a drug addict — she was an alcoholic. It had begun innocently enough, just the odd glass of beer when she was a toddler. Everyone found it amusing when little Leigh got tiddly by sneaking sips from Dad's can of Foster's — she looked so comical rolling happily about on the floor giggling. Cute. It was just simple kiddy hijinks, nothing to worry about.

Certainly no one made any connection when years later she started to do badly at school; she just seemed to be so tired all the time, probably a hormonal thing they reasoned. By the time she was eleven, she was in serious trouble and nobody knew, least of all her parents. They drank a lot themselves. They weren't alcoholics, they were quick to point out, just social drinkers who liked to entertain. Consequently, they kept the bar well stocked and never noticed when the odd bottle went missing. In later years, when she began to babysit for extra pocket money, Leigh learned to raid other people's liquor cabinets. She never took enough to be caught out, just a nip or two out of each bottle, but this would quickly add up to a powerful cocktail. Normally, she never drank in the house itself; she'd pour the pilfered liquor into a little hip flask, smuggle it out and drink it later. Unfortunately, on the night she babysat Rebecca, she decided to break the pattern.

This aberration had a lot to do with Rick, her boyfriend, who in response to her phone call, had crept into the house about an hour after Jenny and Simon had left. Rick was nearly seventeen and not normally a drinker, but what he had in mind for this evening required some inhibition loosening for himself as much as Leigh. So when Leigh showed him the flask of mixed spirits she'd siphoned out of the Collins' liquor cabinet, he was quick to suggest that they drink it right away. Leigh protested, briefly — despite her alcoholism, she took her job as a babysitter seriously and didn't want to be caught out should little Rebecca need her — but Rick was persistent. Eventually, she weakened and went to find a bottle of Coke. She drank everything with Coke.

In his hormone-driven enthusiasm, Rick had made two serious miscalculations. Firstly, he had no idea that Leigh was an alcoholic who, once she got started, would simply drink herself into oblivion. Secondly, he hadn't anticipated his own reaction to such a powerful concoction of spirits.

After vomiting for what seemed the hundredth time, he hadn't felt vaguely romantic, and even if he had, the slurring, dribbling creature Leigh had degenerated into would hardly have been the object of his desires.

Somehow he managed to carry her unconscious body into the guest bedroom and, after making a valiant effort to clean up the evidence of their impropriety, fell asleep beside her.

In his hand was a lighted cigarette.

About a mile from home Simon heard a siren behind them. 'Police,' he muttered. 'Probably another false alarm at the Baileys'.'

The Baileys lived in a ghastly pseudo-Spanish mansion a few doors up from them and false alarms from their recently installed security system were driving the neighbourhood crazy.

'No, it's a fire engine!' Jenny said.

Simon pulled over to let the stroppy red machine go by.

They looked at each other.

'No. It couldn't be ...' Simon said.

Jenny was praying.

By the time they got home, their house was beyond saving. Two fire engines, a police car, and an ever-growing crowd of onlookers blocked the street. Simon stopped the car in the middle of the road, leapt out and began to chase Jenny who was already racing towards the flames, screaming. It took two very determined firemen to stop her from hurling herself into the inferno. The heat was incredible, she would have been incinerated well before getting anywhere near the house. She thrashed about in their arms and between sobs tried to tell them that her baby was in the house. They did their best to calm her, but could offer no comfort — whoever was in the house would have died a horrible death. The firemen already knew Rebecca and Leigh were in there, the neighbours had told them that. At this point, no one knew about Rick.

Simon stood off on his own, completely gutted. He watched the fire suck the oxygen out of the night and the happiness out of his life.

In his mind he could see a little girl with her mother's eyes, running towards him. She was laughing. In her hand she held something tiny — a shell? No ... a crab, a hermit crab. He wanted to tell her about that crab, he wanted to tell her about everything.

He cursed God and he wept.

Then the heat and the suffocating smoke brought him

back to the present, forced him away from the pyre and back to Jenny. He put an arm around her. There was nothing to say.

Mrs Asakura, the quiet Japanese lady from across the road, put a blanket around them. Two cups of hot sweet tea appeared from somewhere.

Jenny didn't appear to notice any of this; she continued to stare trancelike as the fire slowly succumbed to the firemen's hoses.

Simon buried his face in her hair and smelled Rebecca there. His mind was filled with her happy soft chuckle, her curious eyes, her promise. Grief wracked his body.

After what seemed an eternity, a fireman emerged from the smoking, puddled, black bones of the house and walked towards them. He was exhausted, shocked and covered in soot and water. He couldn't imagine a worse death than being burned alive; he never got used to it. Unable to meet their eyes, he walked past them and in a trembling voice reported his findings to a senior fire officer and a policeman who stood a little way off.

'We've found two bodies,' he said as quietly as he could.

Jenny let out a silent sob.

'Both teenagers, I'd say,' the man continued. 'One'll be the babysitter and the other's her boyfriend, I reckon. They were in the bedroom ... on the bed. Never had a chance. Looks like the bed caught fire — a cigarette probably.'

'Or something stronger,' the policeman added a little unnecessarily.

Simon moved closer. 'What about the baby?' he demanded.

'There's no sign of her in the nursery,' the fireman said, taking no offence at Simon's tone — he had faced the misdirected fury of grief many times before. 'We're still looking. It's a mess in there.'

'She must be in the nursery. Where else could she be?'

'We're looking everywhere,' the fireman said, not saying what was in all their minds — that they would eventually find Rebecca's tiny, charred body in there somewhere.

Quite suddenly, Jenny seemed to lose interest in their conversation.

'Little Yin and little Yang!' she said, as if reaching a decision. 'Simon, we've got to find little Yin and little Yang.'

Simon heard the disassociated tone of her voice. Probably shock, he reasoned, some sort of hysteria setting in.

Others had the same thought. 'Is there anywhere you can take your wife so she can rest?' the policeman suggested.

Mrs Asakura, who was standing nearby washing her worrying hands over each other, nodded and smiled a mother's smile.

Simon put his arm around Jenny and pulled her head to his chest. 'Go with Yuki, Jen, I'll stay here and—'

With an exasperated grunt, Jenny broke away from him and began running down the side of the property towards the back of the house.

The policeman made to follow, but Simon stopped him. 'I'll take care of her. If you want to do something useful, why don't you do tell these bloody ghouls to push off,' he said, sweeping an arm in the direction of the faceless onlookers whose presence suddenly seemed obscene.

Some in the crowd were offended by Simon's outburst but the policeman understood. He moved off to do as he was asked.

Searching the whirlwind of his mind for words beyond his experience, Simon went looking for Jenny.

Skirting the steaming, hissing pile of bricks and metal that once was their home, he made his way to the bottom of the garden to where the property backed onto a park. Over the fence he could see the adventure playground with the little swings and slides that Rebecca would never use.

Jenny stood clutching the gate staring out into the darkness.

Simon approached uncertainly.

Behind him he could hear the firemen packing up and the cars of the curious moving away. A few firemen were still wearily searching through the waterlogged ruins.

'Jen,' Simon said, hoarsely.

She turned to stare at him, but said nothing.

'Darling, there's nothing we can do,' he said, moving to her.

'Little Yin and little Yang ...' she whispered.

'They're gone, Jen,' he said, holding her now.

'No, they're not! They're looking after Rebecca. I made them promise.'

'I know, Jen,' he said. 'And they will ...'

'No, you don't understand.'

'Yes, I do, darling, please ...' He tried to ease her away.

'Listen!' she said, urgently, gripping his arms fiercely to hold him still.

'What?'

'Listen!'

He listened: a fire truck was driving away, old Jim from next door was telling somebody about someone called Rick, a dog was barking and ... Rebecca! For an instant he imagined he could hear Rebecca's chuckling, distant and surreal. Then it was gone, just a cruel trick of the mind.

He looked at Jenny as something approaching happiness lit up her eyes. 'You heard her, Si — didn't you?'

He felt tears rise. 'Please, Jen, it's just ... night noises. Birds probably.'

Then he heard it again — the unmistakable chuckle of their happy baby.

Jenny saw his head tilt back like a dog trying to catch a scent. 'It's her, Si. It's Becky, isn't it? You can hear her, too, can't you?'

'Yes ... yes, I can!' he said, sure now that it wasn't the

———

wind, nor birds, nor the wishful thinking of a hysterical mind. He could really hear it — Rebecca's chuckling — coming from the park.

'Rebecca!' he shouted as he threw open the gate and they ran blindly into the park.

Alerted by the noise, some of the firemen came after them bearing torches.

It was one of the firemen who found her — lying in the middle of the sandpit, comfortably nestled in a shallow depression lined with a rug. She was wrapped in a soft pink, woollen blanket and lying beside her, one each side, were two cute, plump, polished wooden figures.

Years later, the fireman would say that the thing he remembered most about those two carved figures was the delightfully serene smiles on their podgy little faces.

Unlike Simon and Jenny, he didn't notice that their tiny wooden feet were covered in sand.

FORGOTTEN HEROES

Billy lay spread-eagled on the imitation Persian rug, his mouth opening and closing as though gasping for air or grasping for words. For an instant his fists clenched and a terrible light sparked in his eyes; then the moment passed and the fight went out of him.

Deprived of a human opponent, Frank began to unleash his fury on the chairs, lampshades, pictures, pottery and other furnishings that filled that innocent room. When he began to attack the walnut-veneered china cabinet she'd inherited from her mother, Mary began to cry.

Slowly, so as not to attract attention, she went across to comfort Billy who had climbed unsteadily to his feet. Together they moved to the safety of a doorway where they stood and watched her husband and his father destroy the things he'd worked so hard to give them.

Minutes later the front door flew open and released Frank into the night.

A blind rolled up at number 47 to reveal the vulture-like form of the neighbourhood gossip, Clarissa Cromwell, squinting out into the street-lighted gloom.

Frank picked up a lump of dirt from his garden and hurled it towards her prying silhouette.

The clod of dirt burst harmlessly but noisily against the window and sent Clarissa shrieking back into her living room to bully her husband from his fireside dreams.

After a time of angry walking, Frank found refuge in a group of ancient oaks that clung to the shoulders of an extinct volcano that loomed above the sleeping suburbs.

He sat heavily and gazed out over the rows of green, blue, white and orange lights that crisscrossed neatly all the way to the horizon — an illusion of order in a world of chaos.

The kids of today, why is it they always have to know everything? Always questioning. Never satisfied. No patience. It all has something to do with too much money, nuclear warheads, computers, junk food, corrupt cops, bullshitting politicians and all the other space-age crap we've got to put up with these days. What was it he'd read recently? The world was about to enter the 'Information Age'. In other words, like it or not, everybody was going to be flat-out minding everyone else's business. And somewhere, in some featureless building protected by electronic eyes, there lurked banks of computers that knew more about you than you knew about yourself. Everything! From the day you are born until the day you die. And they store those things, for ever — especially the crimes.

He wondered if they knew about him and Mabel Stanistreet that long ago summer — she said she was sixteen, but he knew she wasn't.

That was life for him back then — girls, rugby, beer. Work hard, play hard, the important thing was to keep busy. Broader issues like running the country, or the world, were the business of older folk. You trusted them, you respected them, and — if you were a spotty teenager — you certainly didn't question their judgment. Not out loud, anyway. In fact, Frank couldn't even remember being a teenager, not in the laid-back, far-out, anti-every-bloody-thing way the kids were today.

It wasn't as if he were an old man, but for all he had in common with the kids who slouched around the streets propping up walls these days, he might as well have been a hundred.

Nineteen hundred and sixty bloody eight! For some, the sixties had been a time of change; for him it had been a time of panic. His ideals hadn't just been challenged, some were openly reviled — especially by his own children. This endless bloody Vietnam War argument with Billy was typical.

They may have shared the same blood, but the differences in their upbringing had made them strangers.

When Frank was fifteen he'd left school to take a job in a timber yard. Just getting a job seemed enough; nobody talked about job satisfaction. The thing was to get a job and work like hell to keep it. Earning wages to help out at home was important, too. Not that it was asked of you, it was never really discussed; you just did it as a matter of course and with a degree of pride.

He didn't expect his own children, Billy and Debbie, to do this. He'd wanted their life to be easier and he worked hard to make sure it would be.

He loved them.

In the beginning, they loved him, too — spontaneously and unselfishly. He remembered how they'd rush out to meet him at the first squeak of the front gate that would announce his arrival home. Shrieking excitedly they'd fall upon him, their tiny fingers clutching at his trousers, demanding to be swept up into his arms. He'd loved them so much that just holding them close like that stirred up such a fierce pounding in his heart it almost took his breath away.

Slowly, almost imperceptibly, things began to change. As they grew older they found more important things to occupy them: school, sport, friends, television — diversions that became far more attractive than waiting to welcome home a father who came and went each day with monotonous predictability.

When it became clear they'd never be rushing out to greet him with tales of everything that had been important in their day any more, he finally oiled the squeaky front gate — something he'd deliberately avoided doing for years.

Then, when the children were old enough to take care of themselves, Mary took on a full-time job. Initially, she did it to help out with the finances, but it soon became more than that. She loved the stimulation of the workplace, she thrived in it and would never happily accept a housewife's role again. In many ways Frank was happy for her — the extra money was certainly welcome — but another part of him missed being the centre of her world.

It was around this same time that his relationship with the children suddenly became strained and uneasy — almost antagonistic. He never really understood how it happened. It was as though he'd gone out for a long walk and returned to a house full of strangers. Now, instead of being the father they loved without question, he found himself in the role of rule maker and disciplinarian, the one to be feared or challenged according to mood or circumstance. Wide-eyed adoration was replaced by narrow-eyed petulance. Now, far from being grateful for the little he could give them, they came to expect it — as if it were their due — and if he ever failed to provide what they expected of him, they never failed to show their disappointment. At first, this only made him more determined to be a better provider; but when their disappointment gave way to disapproval, and finally to sheer truculence, he began to realise he had created a monster.

He'd tried reasoning with them, tried telling them of the hard times he'd known as a child during the Great Depression, hoping they'd see how well off they were in comparison. It had no effect. They either couldn't or wouldn't relate to his past; they only cared about their present and the fact that other children had more money, more clothes, more travel, more of everything.

Confronted by this self-serving attitude, Frank's powers of reason often deserted him. To him, their disrespect and ingratitude amounted to betrayal. So he fought back clumsily, with anger and sarcasm, as if by belittling them he might devalue their opinions.

Naturally, they misunderstood his outrage; they could not know that he was hurt more than angry, they saw only that he appeared to despise them. The gap between them widened inexorably. Now he was terrified he had lost them altogether and was haunted by a chilling sense of failure.

The truth was, despite what he told the children, Frank didn't remember his childhood as being much of a hardship at all. Looking back it was easy to see just how poor they must have been, but he'd been born into poverty and for the first few years of his life it was all he'd ever known, so there was no sense of loss. He couldn't even remember being hungry. He knew, now, that his parents must have gone without, but somehow they always managed to feed and clothe their children. The food was basic — bread and dripping, soup, and the occasional rabbit stew, and Frank's clothes were always ill-fitting hand-me-downs, but he was happy, warm and loved, and that is what he remembered most.

Sometimes, at night, in the moment before sleep, certain memories would catch him unawares — his parents in hushed, desperate conversations, their momentary unguarded looks of helplessness, the slump in his father's shoulders — stark yet elusive images that would linger in his mind as sharp and clear as if it were happening at that very moment, then disappear as quickly as they came.

Lately, however, these memories were becoming increasingly confused with images he'd seen more recently in books or television documentaries. Now, he wasn't sure whether he'd ever actually seen his mother stealing coal and his father queuing for work, or he'd just put their faces into someone else's photographs.

Nevertheless, he had known nothing of the luxuries his own children enjoyed today, of that much he was certain.

He was also certain that he didn't agree with this conscientious objection stance the kids were taking against the Vietnam War. What kind of bullshit was that?

Frank could still remember the incredible sense of disappointment he'd experienced when, despite volunteering to fight the Japs, he'd been rejected for military service on medical grounds. Twenty-eight years old and strong and healthy in every way except for a stupid hearing problem that had kept him at home. He felt cheated. While others died for their country, he spent the war working alongside women in factories. The sense of shame sat on him like a stain. When the Americans dropped the bomb and Japan surrendered, he stood by the roadside to welcome the homecoming heroes as a mere spectator. His one chance for glory had gone for ever.

The sun found him stretching, yawning and investigating the world through red eyes. His body — aching from an uncomfortable night on cold, damp earth — took a while to find itself. The day smelled good. The sun was warm on his face and for a time he toyed with the idea of staying in this perfect place for the rest of the day. Then a jogger invaded his solitude with the rasp of tortured breathing. Frank looked at his watch — he had plenty of time to get to work. He brushed the dirt from his clothes and shuffled off down the hill.

As he walked he thought of Mary. She would be worried about him, still angry no doubt, but worried nonetheless.

For the first twenty-three years of their marriage they had never really had a serious argument. Even as their relationship had gradually degenerated into grudging co-habitation, they had somehow managed to avoid the unpleasantness of bitter slanging matches. Perhaps if they had wrestled a few of their problems out into the open, things might have been different. But it was a risk he had never been prepared to take. Not just because he was petrified by the thought of losing her, which he was, but also because he was terrified of breaking up his family. He had long since come to accept that bringing up a family might be the only important thing he would ever do in his life. Caring for them and protecting them gave him a sense of achievement and self-respect. He wanted to tell Mary that, wanted to hold her in his arms and tell her how he could feel his family, his life and his pride slipping away and how it scared him to death. But somewhere along the way he'd forgotten how to talk to her and she'd stopped listening.

He tried to think of her the way she was when they first met, tried to capture the smile, the way she laughed at his corny jokes, how her eyes would widen with excitement at the plans they made. They were happy then. Perhaps not dizzily in love in the romance novel sense, but what they had seemed stronger somehow, more permanent — invincible.

Once they had been the best of friends but now they were separated by a distance neither knew how to cross. Whatever passion she had once felt for him had long been replaced by the kind of love that people have for pets. She took care of him, prepared his meals, kept his house, kept him company and, until very recently, had always been faithful to him.

Faithful! What a bloody joke. Dear sweet innocent Mary,

mother of my children, grunting, sweating, smiling — spreading her legs for some expense-accounted prick years younger than her.

He'd tried to understand, but couldn't. He'd tried to leave her, but couldn't. He'd tried to hate her, but couldn't.

It amazed him how everyone had known what was going on except him. Even Billy. It was ironic really; whenever Frank had seen this sort of thing happening to other people he'd always wondered why the betrayed party was always the last to know. He used to think they must be blind or stupid not to notice. Now he knew better.

More lies: she still loved him, it was just that she'd been a virgin when they married and she was curious to know what it was like with another man; it was his fault as much as hers, he'd been drinking too much and lost interest in sex; she needed to feel wanted again. Bullshit — all of it!

More by habit than with any real sense of purpose, he clocked in and found his way to the Dispatch Department where he hung up his jacket, donned a dustcoat and attempted to check the day's first deliveries. It was futile; his eyes wouldn't focus. All he could see was Billy, hands on hips, shouting at him.

'You don't give a rat's arse about what's right or wrong, just how brave you all were back in good old World War Two!'

'Yeah, well, thank Christ we didn't have to rely on you and your gutless long-haired mates back then.'

'That was then, this is now. The world's not at war now.

Why would any sane person want to send their sons away to be scared shitless in someone else's war?'

'Everybody's scared in war. It takes real courage to do the right thing when you're scared.'

'What's *right* about napalming innocent villagers?'

'They're napalming jungles, not villages. No one wants innocent people to get killed, but that's war.'

'Win at all costs, eh? Fuck the morality.'

'At least the Yanks have the guts to fight for something they believe in.'

'Get off the grass! Half the poor bastards are drafted. They join up or they go to jail. Some choice. Anyway, what are they fighting for?'

'For freedom, against communism.'

'Oh, the dreaded *communism*! Some poor bloody poverty-stricken peasants want some kind of equality in their own country. Well, shit, we can't have that, can we? Much better to kill off a few hundred thousand children than let them turn red!'

'They don't *want* to turn red, that's the whole point.'

'How the hell do you know? How many Vietnamese have you spoken to lately?'

It was a futile argument. The real reasons for the Vietnam War were as much a mystery to them as they were to most people.

Frank kept getting it confused with the Korean War — Asia, north versus south, communism versus democracy, America backing the good guys. Okay, so this time it wasn't a popular war, lots of people were questioning it, not only the young. But the world has always had its share of socialist bastards. The way Frank saw it, if the Americans believed there was good cause to be in Vietnam, then New Zealand should be there, too. America was the guardian of world democracy and New Zealand was their ally. That's the way it would always be.

He was going to say something along those lines when he saw Billy's eyes light up, as though he smelt victory and couldn't wait to taste it.

'Have you ever noticed how every time a bomb kills a couple of people in Ireland, the newspapers are full of it?' he said.

'What the hell has Ireland got to do with anything?' Frank answered cautiously.

'Everything. A couple of Irishmen getting blown away is chicken shit compared with the hundreds, perhaps thousands of Vietnamese that get killed every day. But do we hear about them? No way! Why? Because they're only little yellow people, that's why. Just slopes and gooks. It's not like *real* people are getting killed.'

'Jesus Christ! You're not trying to tell me it's a racist war!'

'Well, *isn't* it?'

Frank was not a racist, not now nor ever. He resented the accusation. He was sick of the boy's lack of respect, up to *here* with his smugness and his ingratitude. He worked his arse off to give this spotty prick a good life and all he got in return was this namby-pamby bullshit.

'The *truth* is that all your conscientious objection crap is just a cover-up for the fact that you're just plain gutless. A bloody nancy boy!' he said.

For a moment Billy stood stunned. Slowly, he gripped the headrest of the couch, his voice shook.

'Well ... if you're such a hero, why's Mum leaving you?'

'You fuckin' little—' Frank choked as he lurched towards him.

The boy stood his ground, defiantly. 'Go on, hit me. Show me how brave you are, you pathetic bastard.'

Mary ran in from the kitchen. 'Stop it! For God's sake.'

'Tell him, Mum, tell him!'

Every Anzac Day, Frank attended the dawn parade. In the beginning he hadn't taken part because, despite his wishes, he hadn't ever been in the forces, so he just went along to show his respect. He couldn't remember when, or exactly why, he began marching in the parade itself. It wasn't premeditated, it just happened. He simply drifted into it. He was, after all, around the same age as many of the veterans, and although he had no medals to wear and belonged to no regiment, his presence at the wreath-laying ceremonies seemed right and proper. No one ever questioned his right to be there and with the passing of the years he subconsciously took on the role of an old soldier to such an extent that, in his heart, he became one.

So each Anzac Day he took himself to the dawn parade held at the cenotaph in front of the Auckland Museum. The museum sat on the crest of a hill in the middle of a huge park, and its dignified floodlit facade provided a fitting backdrop for the annual gathering of old soldiers and their memories. In such a setting Frank never failed to experience an intense feeling of belonging, a much needed rekindling of his flagging patriotism, and an almost religious sense of pride in being a New Zealander.

Then, two years ago, this changed.

It started out as a dawn parade like any other. Many familiar faces were there, and a few more were missing — age was their enemy now. Their heads were bowed in silence, each of them alone with their memories.

Suddenly, a group of anti-war protesters ran screaming out of the mist and began to bombard the bewildered veterans with flour bombs.

Some of the old soldiers ducked for cover, others tried in vain to battle their attackers, but the speed and vigour of youth was too much for their tired old bones.

In the chaos, Frank caught sight of an old man standing proudly to attention as if oblivious to the madness around him; a survivor of two wars, he was once again refusing to leave his post. His face was splotched with flour, tears etched down his cheeks; two of his brothers had died so the world could be free to throw flour bombs at old men.

Frank saw red. He ran towards the jeering protesters and began lashing out. Somehow he managed to catch one of them with a kick to the stomach. The force of it felled them both. Frank was first to recover. Rolling to his knees he straddled his prisoner and raised his fist. Then he stopped in amazement — the face he was about to crush belonged to a girl.

'Shit,' he panted.

With the weight of him on her, the girl fought for breath.

The fight went out of him. 'Are you okay?'

'I think so,' she wheezed uncertainly. 'It would help if you got off me.'

He felt embarrassed and slightly ridiculous. 'Sorry,' he mumbled, climbing unsteadily to his feet. His suit jacket was torn.

She made no effort to move.

He offered her his hand.

'Thanks,' she said and grunted quietly as he helped her to her feet.

Still dazed, she swayed towards him. He held her gently at arm's length while she regained her senses.

A pasty-faced youth ran up to them. 'You okay, Shaz?'

'I'm fine,' she said stepping away from Frank. 'Where are the others?'

'They've buggered off. Someone called the cops,' the boy said, nervously shifting from one foot to the other.

'Too gutless to face the consequences, eh?' Frank said.

'Get stuffed!' the boy said and attempted to pull the girl away.

She resisted and smiled apologetically at Frank.

He tried to respond.

She held out her hand. 'Sharon,' she said.

Uncertainly, Frank accepted her hand. 'Frank.'

'I'm sorry about all this,' she said. 'It's only that, you know ...'

She wanted to explain and Frank wanted to understand, but the boy was becoming increasingly anxious.

'C'mon, we haven't got all day,' he snapped and walked away.

Sharon shrugged helplessly, then went after the boy.

Frank watched until they disappeared into the trees.

They didn't look back.

Slowly, the veterans formed back into ranks, the dignitaries took up their places and the ceremony recommenced as if nothing had happened — as if to acknowledge the incident would give it credibility.

Nevertheless, try as he might, Frank could never forget. The injustice of it smouldered inside him still. It confused him as well — because from that day on, whenever he tried to remember Sharon's face, the only person he could ever see in his mind's eye was Billy.

The day moved on relentlessly, deliveries came and went, forms were filled, goods distributed, the work got done. Even in his detached state Frank handled it all with his usual efficiency. On any other day he would have felt a measure of pride in his rock-like dependability; today he felt nothing. Not even the usual parade of drivers with their light-hearted banter and endless grubby jokes could lift his mood. Somehow the security and routine of it all seemed like a lie. He was sick of the lies: a happy family, love, respect, patriotism, a sense of duty, a sense of pride — lies, all of it.

'Pearson wants to see you, Frank!'

Frank looked up to see a chubby pay clerk, standing beside him rubbing his hands together worryingly.

'What for?' Frank asked.

'Buggered if I know. Probably got a rise, you lucky bastard.' The clerk smiled and waddled off in his fat-arsed important way.

After seconding one of the brighter storemen to hold the fort, Frank made his way to the office, wondering what Pearson, the new General Manager, could possibly want. *Rise, my arse*, he muttered under his breath. *It'll be more bloody paperwork, for sure.*

The company had been taken over twice in the last four years, each new regime bringing with it a whole new set of procedures and computer-based administration systems, which always seemed to increase paperwork without noticeably increasing efficiency. Not being one to make waves, Frank complied as best he could, although he was less than impressed when all customers and products had been given computer codes, which he found impossible to remember. Computers confounded him. He was still struggling with metrics, which were another bloody nonsense as far he was concerned, particularly weights and measures. If imperial measurements were good enough for the Americans, he couldn't see why New Zealand had to change to some ridiculous European system. *Bloody bureaucrats!*

Pearson had stepped out for a few minutes, so Frank was asked to wait. Obediently, he settled into one of the visitors' chairs and attempted to read a magazine concerning itself with the latest trends and developments in the international whitegoods market. He couldn't concentrate. He was far too fascinated by the goings on around him. The plush premises of the 'inner sanctum', as the office complex was known, were a stark contrast to the frugal decor of the factory proper. For a start it was quiet. There was no need for office staff to shout to be heard above the roar of the production line. Conversations were carried out in polite, hushed tones, punctuated by youthful laughter. Youth — that was it! That was his overall impression of the people in here — youth and confidence. They carried themselves with an assurance that belied their years — almost arrogance, as if they knew exactly where they were going and how they were going to get there. There was also something in the way they looked at Frank that let him know they thought themselves superior to him. He despised them for it and avoided catching their eyes in case his contempt for them might show.

Pearson arrived in a busy flurry of papers, which he

handed to his secretary. 'I want these dealt with by tonight,' he said, and without waiting for any questions, turned to Frank.

'Ah ... Frank. Sorry to have kept you waiting, another bloody emergency, you understand. Come on in,' he grinned, as a spider might to a fly, and waved Frank into his office.

Frank entered uneasily.

Pearson closed the door and went to stand behind his large desk. On top of the desk was a marble pen stand with matching gold pens, a leather-bound blotter, a telephone and a single red folder — a picture of sparse efficiency.

'Sit, please, make yourself comfortable,' Pearson said.

Frank sat in the chair he was directed to; it was smaller, harder and nearer to the ground than was comfortable.

Pearson collapsed into a high-backed leather chair, which rocked back to accommodate the indolent position he adopted.

Frank's chair remained rigid. So did Frank.

Pearson formed his hands into a steeple with the fingertips gently prodding his bottom lip. He gazed thoughtfully at Frank and said nothing.

Frank wondered what was in the red folder.

Finally, as if reaching a hard decision, Pearson leaned forward and sighed. 'How long have you been with us, Frank?'

'You mean working in this factory?' Frank said.

The point of his response wasn't lost on Pearson, who

had arrived only eighteen months ago with the latest takeover. He put his elbows on the desk. 'Yes, how long have you been working in this factory?'

'Over twenty years,' Frank said, pushing his shoulders back a little. 'Been here longer than anyone.'

'You must have joined straight after the war,' Pearson said as he looked down at the contents of the red folder he'd now opened.

'A couple of years after, actually,' Frank said. 'Got me first job in a timber yard, then I odd-jobbed around to see a bit of the country, y'know.'

'Mmm ... interesting,' murmured Pearson, although he clearly wasn't the slightest bit interested. He continued to study the contents of the folder with such intensity that Frank found his own eyes drawn to it. He tried in vain to read what was written there.

After much too long, Pearson looked up.

'To be perfectly frank, Frank—' He paused, caught unawares by his unintentional wordplay; if he thought about smiling at it, he wisely didn't. 'I have some rather unpleasant news ...'

Frank didn't hear too much of what was said after that. His mind drifted out to the goings-on outside the window — the traffic choking the road with after-school chaos, the milling grey clouds in an undecided sky.

'*... circumstances beyond our control ...*'

A schoolgirl riding past on a rusty bike, she looked familiar, a friend of Debbie's?

'*... duty to our shareholders ... we reluctantly ...*'

Pearson had a huge pimple above his right eyebrow. A beer bloom, it looked painful.

'*... grateful for your contribution ...*'

The carpet featured repeating patterns of the company's logo. Frank's shoes needed a polish.

'*And a fairly substantial redundancy payment ...*'

'Stick it up your arse!' Frank interrupted.

'Now hang on a minute.'

'Hang on yourself, you smug prick!'

'Look! There's no need ...'

'No need for what?' Frank demanded. 'You and your bean-counting pals march in here with your fancy systems and jumped-up titles and overnight you're all fucking experts. Never mind the people who've been here for years. Never mind all the hard work they've put in to build up this business. It doesn't add up to a bucket of shit to you, does it? It's *business*, that's all. Cut the staff, increase the profits. It's that simple. Nothing personal. Too bad, so sad, see you later, Frank.'

'It's not just you, it's ...' Pearson was trying to get up out of his seat but it rocked and swivelled and refused to let him free.

Frank was on his feet now, leaning across the desk.

Pearson suddenly looked very young and unsure of himself.

'Well, *me* is all I care about, mate,' Frank said. 'Me and twenty of the best years of my life.'

'Be reasonable, Frank.'

'Don't you call me Frank. I'm *MR MOSELEN* to you, sonny.'

'Okay, *Mr Moselen*, you're fired!' Pearson said defiantly, although he twitched nervously as he said it.

Frank swore in disgust and wheeled away.

Alerted by the raised voices, a small crowd had gathered to stare through the glass door. They pulled back as one as Frank threw it open.

He turned back to Pearson. 'The union isn't going to wear this crap.'

Pearson seemed to regain some of his lost confidence. 'We've already spoken to the union. We've come to an agreement ...'

Frank didn't stay to hear any more. He strode out of the office and across the factory floor, oblivious to the roar and crash of the steel presses and the curious eyes of those who had drifted out of the inner sanctum to gaze after his departing form. Some were shaking their heads reproachfully, some giggled nervously, others were plainly embarrassed for him; too few wore a look of sadness or regret.

Someone called out his name but he ignored it.

He swept back into the Dispatch Department, threw his dustcoat onto the floor and fought his way into his battered jacket. Ignoring the questions and protestations of the bewildered storeman he'd left in charge, he jumped down off the loading bay and walked blindly out across the highway, filling the afternoon with the screech of brakes and the cursing of drivers.

Just as he reached the other side of the road, a bus pulled up to deposit some schoolchildren. Without thinking, he clambered aboard and asked for a ticket to wherever it was going.

The driver frowned but took his money and gave him a ticket to the end of the route.

Children chased each other towards tomorrow, mothers struggled home with too few groceries for too much money, old men dug life into gardens, young lovers wrestled in doorways — Frank rode past seeing none of it.

When the bus reached the end of its journey, he climbed down into a strange street in an unfamiliar neighbourhood and walked hard and fast towards the sinking sun until his lungs were bursting and his legs screamed out for rest.

Somewhere in the distance he could hear them calling. The lucky ones who died as heroes with their truths intact, who would never see how the world they fought so hard to protect could so quickly forget them, who would never have to suffer ingratitude, humiliation and a mind-sapping sense of failure, who would never know the impotency of growing old.

It wasn't an unfamiliar feeling, the one that filled him now. He'd experienced it many times before — in tall buildings, on cliff tops and even once on a footbridge over the freeway — the urge to lean that bit too far ... But always, at the last moment, he'd pull himself together and drive the madness from him. Usually, the power of this feeling, the terrible temptation of it, frightened him; now, he welcomed it like an old friend.

A wind from the south chased a ball of paper across the railway platform and teased at his trouser legs. He shivered and folded his arms tighter. According to the surly stationmaster, the next train through was an express that wouldn't stop at this station. An all-stops commuter train would follow shortly thereafter. Frank felt calm and sure. He heard the express coming. He moved to the platform edge. His despair was complete.

Then a little girl came laughing and skipping out onto the platform. Golden-haired and full of life, she'd run far ahead of her grandmother, who was trying in vain to call her back. Shrieking excitedly at the sight of the approaching express, the little girl turned to urge her granny to hurry. She didn't see the edge of the platform. She didn't see Frank.

She fell.

Frank jumped.

The screams of the bystanders were lost in the roar of the passing train.

The carriages clattered away into the distance. No one spoke.

A few white-faced people moved to the platform edge, afraid to see what they might see. Looking down, they saw the figure of a broken man sprawled amongst the oil-splattered litter beside the tracks.

He was very still. A woman sobbed.

Then the man's shoulders heaved and he slowly rolled over to reveal the little girl safe beneath him. They were both crying and holding on to each other as if to life itself.

Frank didn't notice the frightened faces staring down at him. He was staring up at a tiny speck soaring high above. A skylark.

And the only sound in the world was the sound of its singing — old songs for forgotten heroes.

About the Author

Born in Kuala Lumpur, Malaya, to a Chinese mother and a New Zealander father of Swedish/Irish/Scottish extraction, John Hanlon was Eurasian way before it was fashionable.

He was raised variously in a peaceful seaside village in New Zealand, the spice-scented bustle of post-war Singapore, the transported Englishness of a West Australian boarding school and the adventure-filled environs of an iron mine deep in the jungles of Malaya.

Reaching adulthood in Auckland, New Zealand, he trained as a graphic artist and began to earn a living briefly as a cartoonist but mostly as an Art Director in Advertising.

In the early 70's, just as he was morphing into an advertising copywriter, he accidentally became a Pop Star.

A few hit songs and a significant number of awards followed in his brief, four years career as a singer-songwriter before he chose to walk away from the limelight and seek a quieter more private life.

He then spent three decades as a Creative Director in Australia, before returning to live in New Zealand and explore less certain creative pursuits like writing fiction, songwriting and painting.

For more about John and his work, visit johnhanlon.co.nz

Photograph: Andrew Pettengell